LOOKING FOR LAZARO

PSEUDONYMOUS BOSCH

To order additional copies of this book, contact:
Xlibris Corporation
1-888-795-4274
www.Xlibris.com
Orders@Xlibris.com
118180

There is nothing natural about sex.

—Guillermo Cabrera Infante

I

So it's come to this.

That's what he was thinking as he descended the steep hill from Revolución: *So it's come to this.* He walked by the women trolling on the sidewalks in tight pants and leather jackets. They smiled and made a little two-part hissing noise sst-sst to get his attention. There were nightclubs, too, and next to each club there was always a narrow flight of stairs with the name of a hotel above it.

That must be how they worked it here. Funny how every place is different about how they work it.

This was crazy. He was long past the years when it might seem appropriate for a man to test himself. A man his age (and a gringo) on foot in perhaps the toughest neighborhood in North America: crazy. *So it's come to this.* But at his age, it was either something like this or nothing. That's what another voice said: *Either this or nothing.* He kept walking.

He didn't want to take a cab because cabs always figured in the How I Got Rolled stories that were such a part of Tijuana lore. The driver says something like: Nobody goes to Club Frontera anymore. I know a better place; let me take you. Pretty girls very young, you know what I mean? No charge for the ride. I get mine at the other end—

He had almost come here the past New Year's, but he'd chickened out. It had been Y2K: end of the millennium; there had been dire prophecies of technological breakdown. He didn't want to be stuck in the notorious Zona Norte when all the lights went out.

But the street was actually too festive to inspire fear. There were carts selling churros, spitted pork, oysters in the shell and chicken fried in hot oil, all eaten by musicians snacking between gigs. They wore silver-studded suits like mariachis, but their huge white cowboy hats identified their style

5

as *ranchera*, the music of bouncing accordions that even now gushed out of the bars. Despite the traditional nature of the music, many of the lyrics were in fact *narcocorridos*, stories of drug lords and cartel soldiers.

The Frontera was at the bottom of a steep hill. A doorman on a stool outside the entrance watched impassively as he went in.

He was expecting the girls to come out and line up like at the Nevada joints. This place seemed like an ordinary bar; perhaps he'd been misinformed. There were groups of guys at tables, sometimes with a girl or two. The women were mostly seated at the bar. They wore nice dresses, unlike the women in the streets, and their hair had been done up with some care. No one seemed to be doing any business.

The waiters and bouncers patrolled in T-shirts with the club's name on them. He ordered a beer and looked around. He was reassured by the presence of a table full of Asian guys in the corner. Any place where Asian guys hang has got to be safe. A bit later, a couple of uniformed cops walked through slowly, looking around but not stopping.

There was a central dance floor, but no one danced. The guys, mostly gringos and a few Mexicanos, still seemed almost to be ignoring the women, who stayed quietly along the bar or in the alcoves at each end. Not like Cuba, where they came up as soon as you sat down and introduced themselves and rubbed your inner thigh.

After a while, he began to get a read on the joint. Every now and then, one of the guys would get up from a table, walk over to a woman, speak with her briefly, and then they'd leave together.

He began to take notice of a short *chica* standing in the corner. She had a pretty round face with Indian eyes, almost Asian, dark and soulful, and she had long, long black hair that spilled over her shoulders. He thought she was looking back at him, but before he could act, a young Eminem-clone with a backwards ball cap came up and walked her away. So now he had to wait, because he had had his eye on her and nothing else had looked as good.

The table next to his had another solo guy at it, and he'd clearly been there a while, as indicated by the mound of butts in his ashtray. The guy wore a leather jacket and aviator shades and he was looking fixedly at the women at the bar, but not ever making a move. One of the girls on the barstools didn't appreciate this, because she wadded up a paper napkin and threw it at Leather Jacket. Then, when the guy looked away, she tossed another one.

Kaiser knew he was beginning to wear out his welcome when one of the wads landed on his own table. But his baby hadn't come back yet. He decided to check out some of the other joints in the neighborhood. Moulin Rouge had women at its bar, too, but huge ones, *muy gordas*. The Floridita Club around the corner had a Mexican crowd, just a few Anglos sprinkled in, and topless dancers who stood at the bar between numbers, with crude implant jobs that looked like something from a B-horror flick.

Back in the Frontera, he found a seat and saw that his *amor* had come back. He walked over, trying to retrieve the little Spanish he knew for the chat-up prior to *los negocios*.

Buenas noches, he said. *Me llamo—*

Sixty.

Was she trying to guess his age, Kaiser wondered? He hoped he looked better than that.

Huh? he said.

Sixty dollars.

Oh: okay.

That was how they worked it here.

So now he followed her past the check stand, where she informed a woman she was going, and he followed her out of the club and up the stairs. The hotel desk looked like the cashier's booth at a theater; the concierge, a guy with a mustache and a San Diego Padres cap, was behind glass. There was a sign pasted on the window: PRECAUCION CONTRA LA SIDA, below a drawing of an erect condom that measured a good nine inches.

Ten dollars, the desk man said, in English.

He slid the money through the slot in the glass and followed the girl into a long white corridor of tiny rooms.

Rooms, hell. These were cribs, cubicles like the ones in Algren's *Walk on the Wild Side* (not to be confused with the piece-of-shit movie version that had the whores working in a French Quarter mansion). Inside the chamber, there was no brass fourposter, no paintings on the walls, no tall Spanish wardrobe and no antique dresser with a circular mirror. Not even a hook to hang clothes on, just a bed and a bathroom.

He tried conversation again.

Cómo te llamas? He got a look of incomprehension from her. What's your name?

Esmeralda, she said, and she smiled. *Y tu?*

Jack.

Do you speak Spanish?

Un poquito. Where are you from—*de dónde eres?*

Mexico DF. I think you should stick to English.

I get that a lot.

He got that a lot. He had taken one Spanish course fifteen years earlier and apparently hadn't learned as much as he thought he had.

She slid her dress over her head and slipped it over the lone coat hanger, which she hung on the doorknob. For his own clothes, he was forced to make do with the rooms single other piece of furniture, a chair.

Hace frío, she said when she was naked, and she quickly jumped under the covers.

No shit.

He slipped in beside her. He looked up at the ceiling and was pleased to see a fan with wooden blades, one small bit of classic whorehouse decor.

And she was beautiful. He told her so, and he wasn't lying. Her long black hair fell on either side of her tits, which were gently rounded. They had to be real. He sucked on one, then the other. He kissed her belly, licked her ears and her navel. She produced the condom that had been left under the pillow and slipped it on him.

Is OK *la boca*? he asked.

Si te gusta.

In Cuba, not long before, he had made a discovery. He'd been inactive for so long that he'd never gotten used to the new fact of sexual life: condoms. He had no problem getting aroused, but with a rubber on he found it difficult to close the deal. There came a point when you stopped feeling anything, just when you wanted to feel most acutely. The same was true tonight, even with her lips tight around it. In Cuba, they called a rubber a *quitasensaciones*. He finally had to tear the thing off and take matters into his own hands, while she just sat there and watched.

The safest sex of all.

*   *   *

The following Tuesday, back in Los Angeles, he was screening a movie for his Film and Feminism class: *Elephant Walk*, starring Elizabeth Taylor, Dana Andrews and Peter Finch.

On the surface, it's a stock Hollywood romance, directed by William Dieterle, a man with a reputation as a faceless studio craftsman, he told them, but I think it's an undiscovered feminist classic.

After the screening, he began the discussion.

It's the standard Gothic plot: a young woman marries a man whom she doesn't know well, and he takes her to his castle, in this case a plantation in Ceylon, which turns out to be haunted. Remind anyone of another movie we saw?

Rebecca, a student on the first row said. Only this was kind of the opposite, he added.

How so, Tranh?

Well, in *Rebecca* it was the husband's dead wife who haunts the castle. She was a strong woman, and maybe a lesbian. Here, it was the hero's dead father.

In what form does he haunt the plantation?

The elephants. Especially the leader.

Yes. What does the hero always call that elephant?

That lop-eared old bull. The hero's dad killed the elephant's mate. Just like the same father killed his own wife, the hero's mother, by forcing her to come back to the jungle to give birth to his son.

Kaiser said, So in a way the old elephant is simultaneously a victim of the father and a symbol of the father: his aggression, his bull-headedness, his need to dominate the female.

And Kaiser continued about how the elephant pack was similarly linked to the drunken Englishmen, the dead father's buddies, who run wild in the mansion galleries playing bicycle polo and later make obscene noises at the beautiful Ceylonese dancers who come to perform for them.

It's the rape of the women and the rape of a culture at the same time, he said.

*   *   *

As he was checking his mail in the department office, he heard the secretary say, That's him now, and behind him he heard a female voice.

Professor Kaiser?

He turned around.

Yes, I'm Jack Kaiser.

I'd like to add your class.

She was a small brown girl who, like many of the *latinas* on campus, had tinted her hair a red-orange shade.

It's kind of late, he said. This is the end of the second week already.

He didn't like to add people after the first week. They usually turned out to be problem students.

I've had trouble at work. My schedule was changed without warning.

I'm sorry. I've got a full boat. You can talk to the office people at admissions. If they put you in the class, I'll accept you, but I'm not giving out any more adds.

That would get rid of her. The teachers were usually given total discretion as to whether they wanted to add new students, and it was very rare for the administration to overrule them, except in cases where the student could plead a dire emergency.

*   *   *

He looked around his apartment and shook his head. It was as bad as the landlady said: a great mess of papers, computers and stacks and stacks of books. It wasn't that he was becoming sloppier, it was that time was passing so much more quickly now that he'd turned fifty. The years shrank. Next thing you knew, it was two months since you'd cleaned between the bathroom tiles.

He would have to engage a cleaning service. But he hesitated. It wasn't that he minded paying the money. It had to do with gender (the cleaners would certainly be women), race (the cleaners would certainly be *latinas*), and class. In the South where he'd grown up, his family, like many white families, had employed a black household servant. Kaiser had taken a silent vow that he would never hire house help. The situation led to racism. It was that peculiar intimacy between householder and domestic servant that was so insidious: on the one hand, the householder fancied him/herself closer to the servant than the usual employer. But as a result of this, the householder would ask extra things of the servant and speak to the domestic disrespectfully in a way that a boss in a workplace never would.

He knew he himself was vulnerable because years earlier, he'd gone back home to visit and he had, despite the best intentions, fallen back into the old patterns of complaining and commanding with Beulah, his family's black housekeeper. When he came to his senses, he gave her a gift of $50, but his faith in himself was a bit shaken. He'd seen friends of his in LA, solid liberals all, fall into the same behaviors with their Mexican help. Circumstances create people, he was fond of saying. Put a person in a position of dominance and he or she would dominate, as George Orwell described in an essay that Kaiser regularly taught, *Shooting an Elephant*, a story of Orwell's time as a policeman in colonized Burma.

But now he really saw no other option. A service called Americlean had left a hanger on his knob offering a trial discount.

Look, the people needed the money from the work. He would just have to be careful and self-aware. He punched in the number and made an appointment for the coming Friday.

*   *   *

He was at the front of the classroom, looking over his notes when the small woman from the day before walked in.

This is what you wanted.

She handed him an administrative add-slip, compelling him to admit her into the class. So you sold it to them, he thought. What a little hustler. Have to keep my eye on you. He read the name on the slip: Veronica Tafuliya.

He was a bit disconcerted that he couldn't place the ethnicity of the name. He had become very proficient at doing so here at mightily multicultural Bay City College. Veronica usually indicated a latina, but he couldn't do anything with Tafuliya, which didn't sound Spanish to him. Despite years at the game, he couldn't deduce her nationality. Her appearance was no help, of course, because the majority of students had that same pan-brown complexion and dark eyes.

He looked at her, now seated at a desk in front of him. She smiled and flashed a mouth full of copper-colored braces. Was it really a smile of wicked triumph, or was it just the metal that made it look that way?

She's so fuckin' ugly, he thought, and he was surprised at the thought. He was usually so good at seeing his students the way they liked to see themselves. But there it was again: She's *SO* fuckin' ugly.

*   *   *

That night, he grabbed a sushi dinner at the little place in the outdoor mall. He had done the same thing the night before, but he was still trying to squeeze off a couple of pounds that he'd gained over the weekend. Afterwards, he went to the candy shop two doors over. It was one of those by-the-pound places where you pick your candy out of big jars and weigh it in front of the cashier. All he wanted were two Hershey's kisses, one plain and one almond: he'd found that a couple of candies, just enough to get a taste of something sweet, made a nice substitute for a real dessert.

He laid the candies pling pling on the scale. The counterman, a skinny brown fellow with thinning hair and the name Hahsaan pinned to the chest of his red uniform, looked up at him with a little smile and said, You were in here just last night weren't you?

And of course the familiar little alarm bell went off: Hahsaan is homosexual. Jack Kaiser nodded without returning the smile and left. Years earlier, he would have gone back to the store the next night and bought candy again just to prove he wasn't a homophobe, but age had diminished his need for such trials. On the way home, he stopped at a Savon and bought a whole bag of Hershey's kisses so he wouldn't have to return to the candy store if he craved them again.

Of course, the familiar little alarm bell didn't always tell the truth. He himself sometimes set them off. Once on a flight to MLA, the year-end conference of English teachers, he found himself seated next to a fellow conventioneer. This guy had just gotten his Ph.D. in Composition/ Rhetoric and was interviewing for a job at an LA school, so he asked Kaiser what living in LA was like. After some discussion of sports and restaurants, the talk turned to theater, and Kaiser mentioned that with so many good actors around, LA had finally turned into a good theater town, and that often shows opened there to prep for Broadway.

Like which plays?

Well . . . *Angels in America* was the one that first came to mind, a play about AIDS and the late Roy Cohn.

Slam! The rhetorician took the reference to *Angels* as code that Kaiser was gay and that Kaiser was checking him out, hoping for return of serve. The rhetorician's head jerked around as he was seized with a sudden desire to study cloud formations outside his window.

Kaiser tried to continue, mentioning that August Wilson's *Seven Guitars* was also in town currently, but it was too late. The rhetorician didn't say two words the rest of the flight.

Kaiser found this amusing, but ruefully so. He had to admit that had the roles been reversed, he might have behaved in the same way as the rhetorician.

Another time, still in grad school, he had been grousing with the graduate advisor, a cheerful woman who knew he'd been a screenwriter and liked to talk movies. He'd mentioned that Helen Mirren was a middle-aged guy's dream piece of ass, and the woman had stared at him in sudden indignant surprise, as though he'd slapped her. Then he realized: *She's always thought I was homosexual.* And people hate to be disabused of these little preconceptions; it shatters in an elemental way their faith in their own judgment. The woman didn't recover her composure for the rest of the conversation, just kept looking at him with arched brows and a frown. As with the rhetorician, he wasn't sure he would have managed better had the roles been reversed.

II

Though he had walked away from the Frontera feeling it had been a one-time experience, there he was again (So it's come to this) making the descent from Revolución, going past the chubby women in the too-tight slacks, the wagons with churros and spitted meat, and the ranchera music bouncing out of the raunchy clubs.

Why couldn't this be more like Cuba? In Cuba, things were so much less . . . professional. His first night in Havana, he'd arrived at four AM. Even for a late night city like Havana, it was after hours. The streets were mostly quiet. The government tourist service had placed him in a Vedado hotel whose lobby featured chintzy Romanesque statues set in grottos in the wall, all of which spelled class to the American mobsters who'd originally built the place.

As he stood at the desk checking in, a dark, pretty woman in a black halter and slacks, looking for all the world like a hotel guest and not at all like a hooker, silently walked past behind him.

He jumped three feet in the air. She had goosed his ass.

*   *   *

The Frontera was crowded this night; there wasn't a table open and you could hardly move about. The place was full of young, short-haired gringos in T-shirts and ball caps and their older countrymen, usually bearded and biker-scuzzy. He squeezed in at the bar next to one of these bearded dudes who was chatting with one of the girls, periodically sipping the Corona that he held at the end of a tattooed arm. A group of guys were trying to make their way to the john; Kaiser squirmed to avoid sharp elbows in his guts and feet pressing down on top of his own.

Oof.

I know what you mean, the biker said. I never seen it this packed before.

Is this a holiday?

You might say. Been a holiday all year in San Diego. Everybody's got money to burn. Frankencomm money.

Kaiser had heard plenty about the wireless communications firm that had experienced a financial explosion, riding the tech tidal wave. Apparently many of the guys in here had some connection to it, including the bearded guy, who turned out not to be a biker at all but a communications engineer, working in R&D.

You seem to know this place pretty good.

Ayeh. Been' comin here for thirty years. It used to a lot more Mexican—had a brass band. Now they play Backstreet Bullshit Boys.

Globalization.

Got that right.

Who owns this joint?

Who do you think?

Kaiser shrugged.

The engineer leaned close: *Los Brothers.*

Kaiser knew he meant the two brothers who ran TJ's notorious drug cartel. He also had the feeling it wouldn't be a great idea to pursue the matter further in here, so he changed the subject.

I thought all you techies were into virtual sex, he said.

Semi. Here a lot of the titties are virtual, the engineer said. His name proved to be Bob, and he took a hit off his beer.

These girls come in from the country, he said, and as soon as they get a few dollars ahead, they get two things: implants and orthodontic work.

Kaiser had already noticed the metallic gleam in some of the girls' smiles. TJ, among other things, was a mecca for cut-rate dentistry.

Kaiser was looking around the room. As he had noted on his first trip, most of the guys seemed to be in no hurry to pick a girl, drinking and grousing with buddies and postponing the moment of decision. Hadn't Flaubert said the greatest moment in a man's life was just before he picked his girl, when the night was still full of infinite possibility?

But the remark about the titties intrigued him. A lot of the women did show a cleavage that appeared to be enhanced. He had never handled a doctored breast before. He went up to a well-endowed big-boned blonde standing beside the ladies' room.

Sixty?

Sí.

And up to the love-crib upstairs. The blonde's name was Marcia; she was from the DF. She was out of her dress and shoes in an instant.

He lay upon the bed and studied the big breasts that had definitely come out of a bottle. They were contoured like bowling pins, suddenly becoming fat near the nipples.

She slid the condom onto him and then, instead of getting in bed beside him, she stood at the foot, stretched her arms out before her, dived on top of him and began massaging his body with her own, but rather roughly, he thought, without the gentleness of real erotic feeling. He ran his hands all around the fabricated boobs, which seemed tougher and colder than real ones.

She sucked his cock for a bit, then jumped astride it and humped for a while. Then she got up on all fours and motioned to him to get up and go around behind her. He saw she had an orgasmic sunburst tattooed at the base of her spine. She locked her feet around the back of his knees and he could feel her contract around him as he got inside her. Unlike the body-to-body massage she'd given him, he found this genuinely sexual in a bizarre but elemental way he'd never experienced before. For years afterward, he would continue at odd times to recall this moment, long after the memory of more attractive women had faded.

But at the moment of peak excitement, he again experienced a loss of sensation due to the condom, and he had to pull off the rubber and have her finish the job by hand. When he came, the woman smiled with the satisfaction of an obstetrician who has just completed a successful delivery.

*   *   *

So what are we to make of Nick telling Gatsby that he's worth the whole damn bunch of Tom and Daisy's crowd, and then telling the reader just a few lines later that he disapproved of Gatsby from beginning to end? How can he reconcile those two statements?

No hands. Silence.

That's a good answer, Kaiser said finally. Because I don't think Nick can reconcile them. I don't think we can, either.

It's a condrum.

What'd you say, Denny?

I said it's a condrum.

I think you mean *conundrum*.

Laughter from about half the students in the class.

But you're absolutely right, that's what it is. Yes, Alexey; you had a hand up a second ago.

Didn't Fitzgerald make some famous statement about having two opposite ideas at once?

He did indeed. I'm not sure of the exact words, but it goes something to the effect of: The ability to hold two opposed ideas at the same time is the sign of a superior intelligence.

But isn't it the sign of a hypocrite? Alexey asked.

That, too.

*   *   *

Though his training was in literature, Kaiser generally enjoyed teaching Comp, because the readings were generally about current issues, and this gave him an opportunity to talk about things outside of his own field. However, the new student, Veronica Tafuliya, had turned out to be a real chatterbox, with something to say about every essay they read, whether it was relevant or not. He usually was grateful for students like her, because it meant that he had someone who would leap in whenever one of those dead silences descended on the class after a question had been asked. But sometimes she dominated discussion to the point where he had to ignore her raised hand and call on someone else, just to keep the class involved.

Today, he had collected first drafts, which he would look over briefly to see if a thesis and a coherent structure were present. Two days later, he would return the papers with his comments for the students to revise. By now, he was used to the gamut of problems: there were the students who would have a grasp of structure, but problems with grammar and syntax. Others would write good sentences, but lack a sense of form: ideas would be mixed together without sequential development. These were the most common errors.

It wasn't until he got to the paper by Veronica Tafuliya that he found something out of the ordinary. The paper was a particularly blatant case of plagiarism. The class had studied the essay *Girl* by Jamaica Kincaid, in which a mother reels off a maddening list of do-this-don't-do-that rules for her daughter. The student had found an analysis of the essay, and copied most of it word for word. One dead giveaway was that there were no punctuation errors, but even more telling was that after every quote from the Kincaid work, she gave in parenthesis page numbers that didn't match the composition anthology, but rather must have been those in the book the original essayist was using.

The nerve of this kid. And the brazen ineptitude at concealing what she'd done. Fortunately, plagiarism (and Kaiser thought he had a pretty good nose for it) at the school was rare. First drafts were a good way of weeding it out. When he confronted offenders, the student would usually try to beg off by saying they didn't realize how close they were to the actual source. Well, go and sin no more, Kaiser would say. Properly chastened, the student would go home and write a new paper from scratch.

At the next class, he called Veronica Tafuliya out in the hall and confronted her.

This is unacceptable.

I was going to go back and cite the source in my final draft. I didn't know we had to do it in the first draft.

Kaiser had heard that one before, too.

Then it wouldn't be plagiarism, but it would still get a bad grade because it looks to me like you're copying word for word.

You must understand, she said, that I have too much integrity to plagiarize.

In all his life, he wanted to tell her, he had never heard anyone boast that they had integrity. It was a statement the speaking of which refuted itself. But he wasn't sure she would see the irony.

Then go home and write me a paper in your own words, he said.

Still, that integrity remark disturbed him. How could anybody be so fucking shameless?

                    *   *   *

They had arrived at the point in the syllabus where it was time to teach the essay on homosexuality. The Comp reader, though very good on women's issues, had but one essay that dealt with gay themes, and it was a difficult one: an essay on the drag festival Wigstock that metamorphosed into a meditation on the ideas of Stanley Fish, a literary theorist. And this would always raise the possibility of gay students in the class, and as with discussions of ethnicity, the issue of how to frame questions without ruffling sensitivities.

He made a point of not revealing his own sexuality to the class, though if asked (he never was, of course) he would have responded truthfully. He wasn't worried that some in the class might think he was gay. Only once had this ever produced an awkward situation: a male student who seemed to have questions that required a lengthy conference after every class. Kaiser eventually figured out that the questions, which were usually about points well-covered earlier, were a pretext. Fortunately, all classes come to an end.

It wasn't being thought gay that bothered him, it was being outed that he resented. He'd had a number of friendships with guys who turned out to be gay, and just about the time he'd begun to congratulate himself on his own open-mindedness (always a dangerous thing to do), said friend would start to argue for the proposition that Kaiser had to accept not just the friend's homosexuality, but Kaiser's own as well. After the third or fourth such incident, Kaiser felt himself turning into a genuine homophobe. He decided to take the prudent course and avoid dealing with gay men in any but professional situations. He noticed that many of his straight male colleagues, even those who counted themselves among the most enlightened, did so as well.

The Wigstock essay, however, was a good opportunity for any in the class who wanted to declare their homosexuality openly to do so, and he always tried to make the classroom a place where they felt they could speak freely and comfortably. In this class, however, Veronica Tafuliya, as usual, was trying to dominate the classroom discussion.

I believe that gay people should have the same rights as straight people.

Quite so, Veronica. But the author is taking it for granted that all of his audience already believes that. He's assuming that anti-gay people aren't even going to read the essay. Instead, he's concerned about the explanations for homosexual behavior. How does he contend that homosexuality is usually explained? Oscar . . . yes?

That it's natural. Inborn.

And does he like this explanation?

He dislikes it. He feels like people talk about it like it was some kind of disease or something. They pity him.

Right. That's important, because we usually don't have respect for people whom we pity.

Veronica again: I believe we should be sensitive to the problems gays have to face.

This was how it had been lately. She was always dragging the discussion back to square one. Ever since he'd busted her.

The writer wouldn't disagree, Veronica. It's just that he's got other fish to fry, if you'll pardon the pun. Instead of the natural explanation for homosexuality, does he even offer another theory? What effect did he say the drag queens had upon him? Louise?

He said they made him question his ideas about truth. It made him see how our prejudices shape everything that we see.

I think that's the key. He came away with questions about everyone's assumptions, including his own. I can give you an example of someone you might know who provokes the same kind of questions: the basketball star, Dennis Rodman. When a macho star athlete shows up dressed in a wedding gown, you at first think he's exposing some hidden feminine side. But by having the courage and audacity to do it at all in a way you could say he's more macho than ever. In other words, it's a condrum.

Some of the class looked at him with clearly puzzled expressions.

What did I just say?

You said *It's a condrum.*

I mean a conundrum. That's the word I meant to say.

A few scattered giggles.

He went on: It's a conundrum. Like the statement *I see said the blind man.* That's a conundrum. The opposed categories of masculine and feminine break down and lose all relevance to—

Are you saying that we shouldn't have compassion for homosexuals?

(*There she goes again!*)

No, Veronica, I'm not saying it. The writer is. Except that's not really what he's saying, either. He's just not looking for compassion.

She grinned and the metal glinted.

She has to be doing this with calculation, Kaiser reflected. This is payback. She must stay up late nights planning it.

*   *   *

He knew he was in trouble a couple of days later when she walked in during his office hours.

I have some questions about my paper.

In fact, Kaiser thought he'd been more than fair to her. He hadn't penalized her for the unacceptable first draft. She had written a solid B paper and that's the grade she'd received. He had appended his remarks saying that this would have been a good first draft, so next time don't waste a draft and put yourself in this position.

This is potentially an A paper.

Kaiser looked it over. There were two problems: an occasional awkward expression, and a failure to clearly relate some of the incidents of the story to the thesis of the paper. Sometimes his grading notations could be slightly confusing, but this time he'd been absolutely clear: the inaccurate words were circled and he'd written *relate to thesis* at each point necessary.

Potentially an A paper, Kaiser said, but it ain't there yet.

The relation to the thesis is clear, she said.

Not to me.

This is an A paper.

Look, Veronica, you'd have a lot more credence if I could be sure you're acting in good faith. But I'm not sure you're acting in good faith because your first draft was the most egregious piece of plagiarism I've seen in twelve years as a teacher. And he felt himself squint, Clint Eastwood style, when he said that word egregious. He was having trouble hiding his anger.

She looked genuinely taken aback and surprised. Has she really been getting away with stuff like this? he wondered. Can this really be the first time anyone's ever called her on it?

Look, you can still get an A if your subsequent papers are good. Your class participation is excellent. Whaddya say a truce?

He extended his hand. When they shook, he felt immediately that he'd made a mistake. Her palm was damp and clammy and he recoiled. She gave him a funny look.

*   *   *

There was no truce. As he walked into class and got set up, he noticed that Veronica quickly broke off a conversation with Deirdre Dinwitty, the girl next to her. Deirdre raised her hand.

Yes?

Are you a part-time or full-time teacher?

First time he'd ever been asked that. No big deal; he often volunteered the information himself. But Veronica was clearly behind this. Amazing for a kid so young: trying to sniff out power-ranking at the school. To determine who was vulnerable; who could be bullied. And in class, she tried to portray herself as such an idealist.

Part-time, he said. That's true of the vast majority of teachers in the department. Almost any English prof you have here will probably be part-time. But in the course of a year, I teach the same number of courses as a full-time teacher and I have the same number of students. I just don't get those long paid vacations.

Some chuckles around the room. But after the class, he wished he'd countered and gone more on the offensive. Said something like: Many of the part-timers here have more impressive resumes than the full-timers. I have a Ph.D., unlike most of the full-timers. I've published several scholarly articles. I also have a Hollywood screen credit. I'm a Jew from Alabama who grew up during the Civil Rights era. I was living in Birmingham when the church was bombed. I lived in the Haight-Ashbury in the 1960's. I'm like James fucking Garner on *Rockford Files*, living in his busted-up old trailer at the beach because he's so hip. I do this because I *like* it.

Why the fuck couldn't they see that?

*   *   *

The housekeeping service sent the maids to his house that Friday. They were, as he had expected, two Mexican women who couldn't speak English too well. It took him longer to prepare for their visit (gathering up papers and dirty clothes, getting everything put away) than they actually spent cleaning. While they were in the house, he went to the library to work. When he came back after an hour, they had already gone.

The place did look better; no doubt about it. It seemed larger somehow, and less confining now that it was clean. The phone rang. It was Americlean, asking how he liked his service. He said it was fine.

Was there anything that could have been done better?

Well, there was still a little grout in the crevices between the bathroom tiles.

Later, he felt bad about this remark. He called Americlean back. There had been a rush to judgment, he said. The dispatcher laughed to hear him quoting Johnnie Cochran. Basically, he was satisfied with the job, he said, and had no desire to get anyone in trouble.

III

He had first gone to Cuba shortly after his fiftieth birthday. He already loved the cigars; he was also curious about the country, and the illegality gave it a special thrill. But he knew deep down that it was the stories about the women that had nailed him. He had been on the verge of declaring his sexual life officially over. Could a last-ditch fling resuscitate it?

Probably not. He wasn't even sure he was going to try. Breathing the rarefied air of academia, he had been too politically correct for too long. Hadn't his dissertation been a post-feminist rereading of D. H. Lawrence?

And suppose the women looked grotesque like American hookers, all sharp points and surgical inflation? Or even worse, like the Third-World famine victims on late night cable TV charity-infomercials, bones sticking through the skin, breasts hanging limp?

His first night, though, a smiling young woman, very cheerful and healthy in a clean, tight purple leotard, casually walked up to him on the street.

Mi amor, she said, grinning. She leaned over to give him a look at her breasts. She was not a famine victim.

No tengo casa, he had to reply. For in Cuba, you couldn't bring them into your hotel. That was how they worked it here. You had to rent a *casa particular* for assignations.

*   *   *

The next day he did just that. He found an apartment across the street from his hotel. On the door, there was a large poster of Pope John Paul, who had recently visited the island. An old woman named Ofelia lived there with her middle-aged son. The room was nice, and plenty atmospheric: it had the classic brass bed, louvered windows, and a high ceiling with a circular fan.

The son did the paperwork for the transaction. He was bald, with big glasses, probably gay. You can bring *chicas* here, he said, smiling.

Still Kaiser hesitated. His hosts seemed friendly enough, but underneath it all, were they really cursing this goddamned *norteamericano* who was down here to whore out the women, just like in the old days before everything changed? And there were the police whom he saw on patrol in the streets, ignoring the girls entirely. Were they waiting to entrap the *yuma*—the Cubans sometimes use instead of *gringo* the expression *yuma* which, despite a lot of arcane theories stating otherwise, is probably simply a slurred form of *E.U.* (that is, Estados Unidos) *man*—confiscate his cash (you had to carry a lot, since your American plastic was no good in Cuba) and throw him out of the country?

He sat in his room in the old hotel, the former American mobster hangout he had come to think of as the Wiseguy Waldorf, smoking cigar after cigar. The mob had owned several hotels in Havana, but this was the one in which the gang soldiers themselves actually stayed. George Raft was the official greeter in the casino. It was this same hotel in which Fredo had stayed in *Godfather II*. Coincidentally, the night before he had left the States, he had watched a TV documentary about one of the most illustrious mobsters, a founder of one of the original Five Families. When the time came for this man's son to be inducted into the brotherhood, he wrote a poem to his dad that the narrator read in full. Kaiser remembered one line especially: *I accept the sins that are heaped upon me.* It meant a commitment to shoulder the bloody burden of the father's crimes. To renounce heaven for the struggle in this world. We fight our father's wars.

But now he was watching Cuban state TV: with Che and Camilo in the mountains, black and white footage of jungle warfare. Had people here been watching these same films every day for the last forty years?

Outside the hotel, girls were taking up positions along the street. One of them saw him looking down at her from his high window. She smiled and waved at him. She spoke and he could read her lips: *Mi amor.*

Still, he smoked and paced the floor. He couldn't bring himself to take the next step. At last, he located within himself a righteous anger. He was barreling toward old age; who knew how long it would be before the prostate started to swell or circulatory problems would have him reading those newspaper ads about erectile dysfunction? Wasn't he entitled to get in a few good pops before the shooting gallery was closed for ever? Besides, goddamit, he had worn a Che T-shirt in 1968, when it meant something. He had bought Huey Newton's book, published when Huey was a fugitive here in Cuba. He had even read the damn thing. He'd paid his dues—

I accept the sins which are heaped upon me.

He was out the door, down in the elevator and out on the street. He walked toward the Habana Libre. The sidewalk was lined with women. He passed on the first few offers he got. Then, coming up La Rampa, a woman forcefully grabbed his arm, and murmured in his ear, trying unsuccessfully to make her voice sound husky and tough: *Hey, we fookie-fookie*, OK? She was an absolute doll, with curly black hair and green eyes. When he introduced himself, she said her name was Yipsy. Her awkwardness was endearing. If she had done this sort of thing more than a couple of times, she sure didn't show it. Successful negotiations followed.

Do you speak Spanish? she asked him.

He answered in Spanish that he spoke a little, but not very well. At least that's what he thought he had said. She looked at him, uncomprehending.

I guess not, she said.

She said she was in her second year at the University of Havana, just a couple of blocks away. This was what college girls here did when they were feeling rebellious, apparently: bed a capitalist tourist. What was she studying?

Business administration, said Yipsy.

He took her to the casa, and Ofelia and the *hijo*, watching TV, bid them good evening. In the bedroom, she stripped down to a pair of homemade red terrycloth panties. She reached into her handbag and took out a prize she was hoarding: a jar of green olives. She popped one into her mouth and offered him one. He was going to say no, but he had a burst of erotic inspiration. He took the olive.

He had her lie down and he slid the first olive along the surface of her belly, depositing it in her navel. Then he sucked it up. She giggled.

They kissed for a while, and then, previews over, the feature commenced. On top of her, balanced on his extended arms, he watched her gorgeous face. He had the illusion that he was looking down on her from some great height, orbiting around her in outer space.

He arched his spine in that way that he hadn't done in so many years but, as if this were some X-rated TV sitcom, his back seized up stiff and jolted him with a sharp pain. He howled.

Are you all right? she asked in English.

Demasiado viejo, he stammered. *Demasiado viejo*.

So she got on top. But this is when Kaiser made his discovery about condoms. He tried on top, he tried doggy-style, he tried *la boca*, and finally limber, he got on top again, but that damn glove always got in the way of his pleasure. At last, he had her jerk him off.

It was the first time he'd been with a woman in years. On balance, he had to consider the evening a success.

When he returned to the hotel and turned on his TV, the state-controlled network reminded him that this was Women's Culture Week. There was a show about women's crafts in Cuba. There were episodes about traditional folk artists from rural areas, intercut with segments about urban women artists. In between episodes, the screen flashed the legend: IMAGINAR UN MUNDO SIN DISCRIMINACIÓN CONTRA MUJERES.

The next morning he didn't shave above his lip and around his chin. He decided to raise a mustache and goatee for the first time in twenty years. He went down to the hotel gift shop right after breakfast and bought three Che T-shirts. Not just the famous frowning Che, but the laid-back smiling cigar-smoking Che as well.

He had been re-radicalized.

*   *   *

So if Cuba's so great, why ain't you there?

The question was put to him by Bob the Engineer. They were sitting at a table in the Frontera, flanked by two of Bob's Frankencomm buddies, Chen and Rajiv.

I'm not ready to go to heaven just yet, Kaiser said. TJ is as much of heaven as I can handle.

You're not serious, said Chen. I mean, doesn't the human rights business bother you?

Oh shit, thought Kaiser, here I go again. This time he should just back off and keep his mouth shut. But like always, he couldn't resist.

That expression human rights bothers me. I mean, isn't the right to survive a human right? The right to medical care? To some kind of roof over your head?

Kaiser remembered to whom he was speaking.

I mean, I've never been to China, he said, I don't know what it's like there—

Neither do I, Chen said. I was three years old when I left.

Well, it's just a damn shame that the so-called free countries have agreed to designate twenty-five percent of the world's population as road kill. That's what globalization means. Americans are the worst. They got no sense of social responsibility whatsoever.

Bob guffawed at that one.

Listen at this guy. He's got the gall to sit here lecturing us about social justice in a Tijuana whorehouse.

Kaiser remembered a question he needed to ask someone, and Bob seemed like just the right person.

Do you know what a Tijuana Bible is?

Sounds familiar. What is it?

I was hoping you could tell me. I was watching this show the other night, a new cop show that is supposed to take place in the thirties or forties. All the men wear those big fedoras and the women wear berets and dresses with big shoulders and crack wise out of the sides of their mouths. Anyway, the detective asks the cop if they found anything in the dead guy's hotel room, and the cop says, He traveled light. There was nothing but some bourbon and a couple of Tijuana Bibles. So I'm thinking: what the hell is a Tijuana Bible?

Pardner, you got me on that one. But it does seem like I've heard that expression before.

But by now Kaiser had his eye on a woman sitting in the niche beside the bar. She had an interesting oval face, like a Modigliani, and her brown hair, coiled tight in a bun behind her head, accentuated the effect. He approached with the magic word *Sixty* and they went upstairs.

He was startled by her nipples. They looked like pencil erasers, so perfectly flat on top that they almost could have been cut to produce this effect. She had a beautiful backbone. After the preliminary necking, she peeled off her white panties and jumped on top of him. They humped frantically for a while and he was thinking, THIS—TIME—I—GOT—TO—COME. But no way. When he peeled off the condom and began to use his hand, she saw what was going on and threw her top leg over his, caressing him with her inner thigh, which he thought was very kind.

* * *

The next day, as he was checking out of his motel, it occurred to him to ask the guy behind the front desk if he knew what a Tijuana Bible was.

But Kaiser thought better of it, because it sounded like something shady and the clerk might feel insulted.

The usual wait to get across the border once was around forty-five minutes, but since the passage of NAFTA, things had speeded up quite a bit. The inspectors had been encouraged to get people through more quickly, so much so that Customs was complaining that far too much contraband was slipping across. They meant drugs, of course, not the handful of Cuban cigars that Kaiser had shoved under the driver's seat. The dogs that inspectors brought around to sniff at the vehicles weren't keyed on tobacco; if they had been, anybody with a pack of Marlboros in his pocket would have been pulled over for a search. So the crossing was usually pretty smooth; the most they ever did at the inspection booth was to ask Kaiser to open his trunk to make sure there wasn't a human coiled inside.

Still, there was always a certain amount of suspense. The irritation of waiting was always compounded by the walk-up peddlers weaving in and out of the lanes with the junk they were hawking: not Mexican crafts, but statues of American cartoon characters and black velvet tapestries of the Last Supper.

Worst of all were the members of an oddball church group, Sacred Heart of the Something, wearing uniforms inspired by the Salvation Army. The all-white outfits had a cross on the breast pocket, brass buttons and a double blue stripe at the cuff. They wore white shoes as well and looked like nothing so much as stewards on the *Queen Mary*. Kaiser suspected they were a cult or scam or both, but today he grinned when the collector walked up to his window, and he slipped a buck into the man's slotted can. He felt the donation entitled him to a question.

Say, you know what a Tijuana Bible is?

A Tijuana Bible? It's the same as any other Bible. The Bible is the word of God, so there's only one Bible, señor.

Don't bet on it.

The light beside his lane turned green; it was time for him to drive up to the booth. He was happy to see the inspector was a man; women were tougher on him for some reason.

Country of citizenship?

USA.

Bringing anything back with you today?

Bottle of tequila.

He pointed to the Herradura on the seat beside him. It was always good to have something to show them. If you said you didn't buy anything on a pleasure trip, it might sound odd.

Go on through, the inspector said.

*   *   *

Between San Diego and San Clemente, the 405 is full of dips that take you down into pleasant valleys, with green hills on one side and tide pools surrounded by great brown rocks on the other. Kaiser's favorite stop was at a small shopping center about twenty miles north of San Diego. In the parking lot was a canvas-topped coffee kiosk which offered a daily quiz: answer the question and win a free cup. Kaiser had yet to pay for a cup of coffee there. Last time, he had surprised the counter person by correctly identifying China as the home of the Hakka people.

Today's question was on the blackboard behind the counter: What is the only African country never to be colonized?

He should have known this easily, but he didn't. For the first time ever, he had to guess.

Sudan?

Behind the coffee bar, a short-haired blonde woman in a big green apron shook her head.

The answer is Ethiopia.

Catastrophe. He had to part with a $1.25 for a Brazil/Colombia Blend. But he seized the opportunity to draw the woman into his current research.

OK. I've got a question for you: what is a Tijuana Bible?

I don't know. What?

I was hoping you could tell me. Being so close to Tijuana and all.

I haven't got a clue.

Double wipeout. This was not Kaiser's day.

*   *   *

In Film and Feminism class, he was showing an episode of *Sopranos* that he'd pulled off TV.

Don't you see, Kaiser said, this one is about the corruption we'll accept versus the corruption we won't accept, and how small a difference there really is. The gangsters are outraged when they find that the soccer coach has had sex with one of the girls on the team. Yet a few days earlier, when they thought he was a hero, where did they take him? Ramon, yes.

They took him to their bar and offered him a—

He paused.

Just say oral sex, said Kaiser.

Laughter.

They offered him oral sex with any woman in the bar.

Right. And the girls in the strip club are somebody's daughter, too, and maybe only a year or two older than the girls on the soccer team. Sometimes not even that old. Every town gets upset when a case like the coach's comes up, but every town has strip clubs just like this one.

*   *   *

For the first time in a number of years, Kaiser felt the need to use the services of a psychiatrist, Dr. Phyllis Gluck. He sat across from her in her office, a high rise near the intersection of Wilshire and Westwood.

I mean, it's a different situation in Cuba. A woman who does that isn't stigmatized the way she is here. There've been studies. The women don't suffer from low self-esteem the way a woman does here. It's not something shameful. You know, in most countries, they have an expression: they call it *the life*. But they don't have an expression like that in Cuba. Because it's never the woman's whole life; only a sideline. One guy I know got taken to a woman's home, and afterward the woman's mom came in and served them coffee in bed and chatted with them. That's not unusual. And Havana's not some third-world hell hole, with the women out there all emaciated with their ribs sticking out, trying to make enough money to eat. The government provides everyone a subsistence. So the girls are free to tell you to get lost if they don't like you. That happened to me a couple of times. I even read a communist defense of the rise in prostitution made by a woman in the Cuban government: these woman don't have pimps or brothel keepers to pay off; they're healthy and educated and empowered, she said.

He paused. I'm rationalizing, aren't I? That's what you think. But the situation in Cuba is different from the classic prostitution in many ways.

How about in Tijuana?

Ah well, yes. That's a bit closer to the traditional model. But even there it's not like Bangkok or the window-brothels in Amsterdam. Those women are true sex workers; it's assembly line sex. But in TJ, the women go with one, two guys a night, tops. They don't live on premises, and they decide when they won't to work and when they don't. And they're really nice—but you think I'm still rationalizing, don't you?

What do you think you're doing? She was a tall, thin woman in a black turtleneck and brown skirt whose curly brush of black hair had recently turned gray.

It's what you yourself feel that's important, she said. Kaiser had always thought of her as being slightly older than himself, but today, after a hiatus of some years, he realized that she might actually be his junior. It was, oddly, the new gray hair that had provoked this observation.

Do you feel that you're rationalizing? she asked him.

Sometimes. I don't know. I mean, I know I'm exploiting someone, that at bottom it's all about money. But there lots of ways people exploit others, and I don't think this is necessarily one of the worst. I don't think it's the most horrible thing you can do to someone to fuck them. That's an American pathology: the confusion of sex and power. There's this enormous rage surrounding sex in this country in a way that you wouldn't see in Cuba or Japan or France or even England.

He paused.

But right now you're thinking, he just uses all this sociohistorical analysis as a justification of his own behavior. Isn't that what you're thinking?

Everyone's political beliefs are to some extent a justification of their personal behavior, she said.

Another thing: isn't a guy entitled to a bit of fun before the equipment starts to fossilize? I've had so little of this kind of fun, and in a few years, I might not be able. The men in my family have a history of prostate trouble, you know . . .

He paused a second.

I'm whining, aren't I?

Dr. Gluck said nothing.

By the way, have you ever heard of something called a Tijuana Bible?

In what context?

In any context. I heard the expression used, but I have no idea what it is.

I'm afraid I can't help you.

A moment of silence.

Look, you know I've been a good boy. My behavior has been PC for years. My dissertation was all about sexual politics. I've always tried to be super-sensitive to gender issues in the classroom. So am I not entitled to . . . haven't I earned the right to . . .

It's interesting that you see this as a question of rights. A right that can be earned. And what do *you* feel? Have you earned that right?

I don't know. That's self-pity talking, isn't it? Self-pity is treacherous. It's ultimately what people use to justify the most horrible actions . . . I mean, just read *Mein Kampf*: full of self-pity.

Why is sex so important to you right now?

Ha. I don't believe a shrink is asking me why sex is important. That's a good one. Well, I guess I feel that I've missed out on something. I want to understand it. Sex that is, not love. Love I don't want.

Why not?

That was my mistake. I believed all the cultural propaganda. You were supposed to want some kind of deep relationship. But I was going against my own nature.

How so?

For me, any kind of familiarity, any sense of domesticity just drains all the eroticism out of a relationship.

But you said you wanted to experience things you'd missed out on.

I haven't missed it, really. I grew up in a very stable family. Parents always at home, dinner the same time every night. So I had plenty of domesticity growing up. But no sex.

*   *   *

In English Comp, it was first draft day once more. Everything was again all right until he got to Veronica Tafuliya's paper. The paper described something called Capital Seminar, a conclave in Washington where bright high school kids learned about the government. On the first read-through, it looked okay. But when he began to examine the writing more carefully, he clearly recognized the language of a brochure or web site. Students didn't write papers like this; at least, he'd never read one. And like her first paper, there were no errors in punctuation, another giveaway.

He was dumbfounded. He'd never had a student to whom he'd given a second chance come back at him this way, with more plagiarism. Never.

This was war, pure and simple.

* * *

After the next class he tried the subtle approach, in order to see if she'd say anything to trip herself up.

How do you know so much about this program?

I was one of the ones selected to go from my school.

Well, this reads kind of funny. There's no actual examples drawn from experience. It sounds like a brochure.

I'll fix it on the next draft.

* * *

On the final draft, she interpolated a description of a typical day, most certainly drawn from personal experience. For one thing, there were the sort of little errors in usage he'd seen on her earlier paper once she'd been forced to use her own words. She'd undoubtedly been to the seminar. But she'd just as surely copied some of the materials she'd been given, and used them in this paper.

There was no point in another confrontation. She had once said she was an admirer of Bill Clinton. Deny, deny, deny. That was the lesson she'd learned from Bill. Hell, maybe she'd actually met her idol at that seminar.

So she thought she was a young lady on the way up, did she? *Looking for a seat / Among the power elite?* Well, she was in for a surprise. The plagiarism was so blatant that he was sure he would catch her now.

He found the web site for the Capital Seminar and read everything it offered, but he couldn't find the passages she had cribbed. There was an 800 number listed, and he called and asked them to send him all available materials.

Meantime, so that she wouldn't suspect anything, he gave her back the paper with an A grade. A week later, when he saw the big blue Capital Seminar envelope in his mailbox, he slapped his thigh. In a few minutes, he'd have her dead cold.

But late that night, after many wearying trips through the pamphlets in the envelope, he had to admit defeat. He could only find one line that had been transcribed exactly. Not enough to hang a case on.

He still knew she'd done it. The brochure she'd copied was undoubtedly an older one, no longer in use. He had no recourse now but to wait and see if he could nab her somewhere further down the line.

IV

It wasn't that he hadn't seen the bad side of Cuba.

On his second visit, everything had changed, at least on the surface. A police crackdown had been ordered. The sexual paradise of a year before was only a memory. The beautiful young girls no longer patrolled the streets of Vedado.

But it was still Havana. The women were there somewhere. You just had to find them. He tried to ask guidance from the man from whom he was renting an apartment, a psychiatrist. (apparently, psychiatry wasn't too lucrative in Cuba: the doctor had to rent out two rooms in his house to tourists), but the man spoke no English at all.

The other tourist in the house was Salvatore, an Italian, also a professor, but of economics, and the second morning he brought an overnight guest to breakfast in the living room: a gorgeous statuesque black woman six feet tall with the cheekbones of a model, whom he introduced as Yasmin. Excellent. The club girls were still around.

*　　*　　*

That night, Kaiser was smoking in the lobby of the Habana Libre in Vedado when he noticed a cute woman with curly blond hair, skintight slacks and platform shoes walk past. So there were some Vedado girls still at it, he mused, wondering how she'd gotten past hotel security, but she got in the hotel elevator and was gone.

*　　*　　*

The next morning, he got up just in time to see Salvatore going out of the house with this very same girl. Be damned! He tried to make himself intelligible to *el doctor*.

Me gusta esta chica, he said. Con Salvatore. *Usted pregunta a Salvatore?*

The psychiatrist looked at him strangely. Kaiser's fractured Spanish had simply confused the man. So Kaiser wrote it out on paper. It was still pretty bad, but apparently the doctor was able to get the crux of the thing, because he winked and nodded. That evening, he found the doctor talking to Salvatore in the kitchen. In the language chaos that ensued, Kaiser was finally able to piece it together that the *chica* was not a Vedado girl at all; in fact, not even a Cubana, but actually another Italian tourist who had come on the plane from Rome with Salvatore, an old friend of his.

Oops.

No ser insulto, was Kaiser's pidgin-Spanish attempt at reparation.

*   *   *

He went to Jimmy's Drink, a disco currently called Club something or another, but still known to everyone by its name in Batista days, the period when it had earned its wild reputation. He got into a conversation with a drunken Swedish guy who'd come to town on a charity mission with medicines that were difficult to obtain in Cuba. How could Kaiser justify this terrible American embargo? he asked. Kaiser told him he was in absolute agreement with him. Fortunately, the Swede didn't ask Kaiser to justify Kaiser's own less-than-charitable purpose in coming to the island. That would have been a more difficult question to answer. They talked about the second Patterson-Johanssen fight, which Kaiser had seen on Classic Sports Channel only a few nights before his departure; the one where Johanssen's leg had continued to twitch uncontrollably for minutes after he'd been kayoed.

Kaiser got up to go to the bar; while he was standing there, someone goosed his ass. The woman who smiled when he turned around was not to his taste. This incident was repeated as he walked across the crowded dance floor. Finally, he took up a position in the row of guys leaning against the wall along the ramp walkway just inside the front door. He was immediately surrounded by three dancing women, all pressing up against him. He heard laughter and turned to see, standing beside him, none other than Salvatore, saluting him with the beer can in his hand. The three dancers in front of

Kaiser were all jockeying for inside position. He picked out the blonde who was rubbing her very nice boobs against his chest.

And a moment later, they were in the back seat of a taxi heading for his place. Sitting there in the dark, periodically kissing his girl, Kaiser realized how badly he'd misread his own feelings when he was young. All those years he had thought he wanted a woman who understood him, who saw him as special and unique. That was what you were supposed to want, all right; but in fact, he now realized that all he wanted in his inmost heart was to be just another guy in the back seat of a cab with his arm around a babe: not unique at all, and certainly not seen as such by the lady.

She said her name was Julie; she could speak a little English. They got out of the car with their arms around each other's waists, like an old couple who've been together a while.

There was the sudden sound of human barking. Like in some noir melodrama, a guy jumped out of the shadows wearing the navy-blue baseball cap of a Cuban cop. He waved his billy and grunt/shouted like a Marine drill instructor.

Now it was going to come down on him. Now he was going to find out how Cubans really felt about gringos who came down here expecting to find a piece of cake, just like they did before '59. Now he was going to see what a police state was all about. If he was lucky, he'd only be deported.

But the cop didn't want him. It was the woman he was after. She was Cuban. Foreigners didn't really exist. The cop barked again and motioned with his club for Kaiser to step away from the woman. Trying to palliate the cop, Kaiser made a weak attempt at humor.

Es mi sobrina, he said.

Su sobrina va a ir a la cárcel, said the policeman, not amused. He gestured with his billy once more that Kaiser should step away from the woman and go inside the building—now! Kaiser realized the longer he stayed and resisted, the worse it would go for the woman. He went inside. The last thing he saw was Julie, imploring the cop, *Por favor no, por favor*.

Well, this was great. Not only was he a sexual exploiter, but now a woman was going to prison because of him. When he awoke the next morning, he calculated that Julie must have been awake for several hours already, cutting sugar cane at one of the rural camps where they reputedly sent women charged with prostitution. He envisioned her swinging a machete, still wearing last night's party dress and high heels, her make-up now smudged and runny in the intense morning sunlight.

In order to take his mind off these events, he decided to take a field trip to the tobacco country of Pinar Del Rio. For this, he had to engage a private car and driver, and it was going to cost plenty. But he sprang for it. He didn't want to sit around thinking about Julie.

A driver was summoned by the tourist desk at the Havana Riviera. His name was Silvio, and he was trained as an aeronautical engineer. Like the psychiatrist, he was another educated Cuban forced into the tourist business in order to make a few bucks. They drove through the Vuelta Abajo, the lower slope where the best tobacco was grown. He saw the gorgeous red mountains and the golden sandy soil of the Hoyo de Monterrey, where the best wrapper tobacco was grown. He took photos of the silky tents strung out across the hills to shade the growing leaf.

On the trip back into town, Kaiser began to learn more about the driver. Silvio had read a lot. They compared notes on Hemingway, Chekhov and García Márquez. After a while, Kaiser felt comfortable enough to talk about what was really on his mind: what had happened the night before.

It wasn't that unusual, Silvio said. Over the years, Cubans had learned how to adjust to the antics of the police. You had to play games, use a little strategy. For instance, you could get out of the taxi a few blocks from the place, walk to the building, then wait inside for the girl to come a few minutes later. And so on.

That night, he went to another club. All the ladies wore the same maroon dress. Maybe blondes were bad luck; he tried a pretty *moreno* named Varya. This time, he had the cabby circle the building a couple of times. No police in sight. He spirited the woman up to his room. Everything went fine, but there was that trouble again at the finish line.

No te gustan condomes, she said, smiling as she worked on him *a mano*.

Afterward, she turned on the TV to see a special holiday concert by several of the top local bands. Kaiser was anxious to learn about Cuban music . . . What's the name of this group? Of that group?

The woman said something in Spanish that he didn't understand, but he knew that basically she had told him to shut the fuck up so she could listen to the songs.

Yes ma'am. He was definitely on the defensive with women after last night's debacle.

The show ended an hour later, and she called a cab. She left him her number in case he wanted to see her again.

*   *   *

The next night, after midnight, he took a cab to Jimmy's. In the back seat, he tapped out the letters I'M SORRY on his pocket translator. The translation came back: LO SIENTO.

Inside the club, he grabbed a beer and went to the place against the wall that he'd occupied last. He looked to see if Julie was there somewhere in the shadows; he didn't have to. Within a couple of minutes, she and a dark-haired friend were upon him like flies on *mierda*, shaking their fingers like scolding schoolmarms.

Your *casa* is no good! said Julie.

You got her arrested, said the friend.

Lo siento, said Kaiser.

Julie held up her wrists to pantomime handcuffs. She pouted.

Lo siento, he said. I'm sorry. What can I do?

We can do it tonight.

But you don't like *mi casa*.

I have a *casa*.

No tengo condom. Estan a mi casa.

Don't worry. I have. And please, speak English. Your Spanish comes out like Portuguese.

So in a few minutes they were in the back seat of a cab again, only this time heading west, out toward Miramar. They turned off Fifth Avenue onto a side street. It was dark; unlit, like so many streets in Havana. Kaiser considered the possibility she might be taking him to get rolled, and he was carrying a fair amount of cash, like most American travelers did in the only country in this hemisphere where their credit cards were worthless. That would be a nice bit of revenge for Julie. But he had resigned himself to taking whatever punishment was coming to him after what had happened two nights earlier.

In fact, things went rather nicely. Turned out they were heading to a little duplex with louvered windows; he recognized the style of south Florida in the late fifties. The house belonged to a very butch lesbian couple from whom Julie rented a room in back. For a while, they chatted with one of the women in the parlor, a middle-aged dyke in sweatshirt and jeans. Julie had told her the story of the policeman already, but now she was saying, *this is the guy*. There was laughter—that was good. Apparently, whatever happened hadn't been so bad. Julie even told how he had said *Es mi sobrina* to the cop. More laughter. He gathered she had been merely cited and released.

The woman left them alone and they went into Julie's bedroom. They necked for a while and then Julie went into the bathroom for several minutes and came out wearing only panties, with her arms crossed over her breasts. She stopped in front of him and flung her arms out wide—TA DA! Like a Tropicana showgirl.

Muy bueno, Kaiser said. Julie was old enough to have a little cellulite on her ass, but was no less attractive for it. Her theatrics continued as they bounced around on her bed, which was a mattress on the floor. He could tell her shrieks and moans were studied. But he was touched that she would fake orgasm for him. That was genuinely sweet. When he pulled off the condom and she had to get him off with her hand, she said nothing. She had seen it all before.

*   *   *

Afterward, there was the problem of getting back to town. This turned out to be hairier than he might have thought. There was the possibility that, while they were waiting for the cab, a cop might drive by and once again bust the Cuban woman for soliciting a foreign man. Strategy was again required, the kind of strategy that he could now see was a permanent feature of every Cuban's life.

The plan was that Julie and the other woman would walk ahead of him together, and Kaiser would hang back as though he was alone. When the two women hailed a cab, the lesbian would peel off and Kaiser would run up and jump in beside Julie. The cabbie wouldn't care; it was only a passing patrol car that might foul things up.

Ay Cuba! the gay woman said, looking up at the sky and slapping her head at the absurdity of it. It was an expression he'd heard Cubans use before, but which he only now fully understood.

So the women set off down the street, and Kaiser padded along behind in the darkness like a faithful hound. He wondered if Julie and the woman were occasional lovers. Why not? They were still laughing and joking, and he couldn't understand a word. He felt like he was a little kid again, following his mother and grandmother through the aisles of a department store as they talked about grownup things incomprehensible to him.

*   *   *

It was in fact on just such an excursion with his mother and grandmother that he had once seen a film called *The Naked Jungle* with Charlton Heston. The film's hook was Heston battling a wave of army ants that was stripping the land bare. Basically, it was sold as a monster movie, and he had enjoyed it as such.

But he'd caught it on late night cable a few years ago and had seen that there was a subtext that had escaped him as a child, a subtext about sex and gender. He recalled that even at age six, the *naked* in the title had made the picture sound kind of nasty. As he told his students after the screening, the real conflict in the movie is within Heston, and it surrounds his attitudes toward sex and women. Heston has built a huge plantation in the Amazonian wilds of some South American country. The movie begins with the arrival of Eleanor Parker as a mail-order bride sent to Heston by his brother. Heston is attracted to her, but as he questions her about her past, he discovers that she has formerly been a prostitute. Heston is caught between his angry, violent moralism and his desire for the woman, which increases with his growing admiration for her as a person.

The ants represent Heston's own repressed feelings, Kaiser argued. And what a terrific visual metaphor: to see him writhing around and slapping at the fiery orange wave. Isn't that a wonderful way to symbolize his internal struggle? He finally beats the ants, but only at the cost of his plantation, just like the Peter Finch character in *Elephant Walk*. Now, cleansed of his violent, angry pride, he can marry Eleanor Parker.

I saw it a bit differently.

Yes, Reshma.

I thought the brown ants symbolized the brown people whom Heston had exploited. What he's fighting is a social revolution, brown waves coming to take back what the colonialist has stolen from them.

Hmm. You've got a point, all right. Heston does indeed go on about how he's brought civilization to the natives. Maybe the destruction of the plantation shows an awareness by the filmmakers at some level that Heston's whole enterprise was corrupt; that his sexual repression was linked to his literal repression of his workers. By the way, did anybody pick up on Heston's sexual history before he meets Parker?

He's never been with a woman, said a male student.

That's right. He's a virgin, and Parker's sexual sophistication puts him at a disadvantage. It threatens his sense of his power, and this is part of what he must deal with. He's been in the jungle since he was in his teens, and he makes it clear he hasn't amused himself with the local girls when he tells Parker: *The Indians have a name for a white man who goes into the villages at night. I was never called by that name.*

A student in the back raised a hand. Kaiser found himself hesitating for a several seconds before calling on him.

Yes, Shao.

What was the name?

We're never told what the name is, Kaiser said, and he realized that he had hesitated because he was sure the student would ask him, *Have you ever been called by that name?*

* * *

His experiment with paid housekeepers had had mixed results. Generally, the work was good, but he couldn't seem to keep a steady crew. After two or three satisfactory visits, his current team would be replaced by two strangers. This meant he had to be there when they came and stick around to give instructions: if he merely left a note, they might not be able to read it.

Why couldn't he keep a steady team? Was he unpleasant to work for? Or was it Americlean? Did their cleaners routinely only stay with the company a few weeks before moving on? He called the company to discuss the issue. They didn't have a good explanation. He couldn't tell if they were being evasive or not.

Maybe he wasn't tipping enough. Though Americlean assured him that no tip at all was expected, he usually put a couple of bucks on top of the check he gave them. Next time he had a good crew, he decided to tip five bucks and see what happened.

* * *

Kaiser held Veronica Tafuliya's paper in his hand. Was now the time to act?

A couple of weeks earlier, he'd given the class their midterm, an in-class essay. Copying a source would have been impossible. He Xeroxed a copy of Veronica's essay before he gave it back. It wasn't a bad paper—the knowledge of the subject was pretty good and the structure was solid but it did have those characteristic writing problems he'd seen previously when she was actually doing her own work: the little mistakes in vocabulary, the occasional slips in verb tense.

The latest paper, on the other hand, had none of these. It was about fraternities and sororities—in itself a cause for suspicion, because there were of course none here at the junior college. Again there was the language of a brochure or web site. And there were no slip-ups in vocabulary, and no grammatical errors, even though this was only a first draft.

He had at first been surprised at how deep his feelings of anger about plagiarism went. But he spent a lot of time, goddamit, trying to be a fair grader. He always took a second look at the low papers, just to make sure he hadn't been in a bad mood. He tried hard, very hard, to strike a balance between being as generous as possible and still being realistic—that is, not being so lenient as to give the students a false impression of the standards that he or she was eventually, somewhere down the line, going to be forced to meet.

He had never had one like this before. He'd never had a student wave it in his face this way. But it would be a tough case if he brought charges. He didn't have her sources.

*   *   *

Kaiser was sitting across a desk from Lucy Kronsky, head of the English Department. Kronsky was a woman of Kaiser's own approximate age who, like many at the college, had never abandoned the styles of her youth as a baby-boomer bohemian: long, straight hair, little granny spectacles and sandals.

I haven't been able to locate her source material, but I think you can clearly see that it's plagiarism.

It's always better if you have the sources in hand, Jack.

I understand. But this is just so egregious. Just read it. It's the language of a brochure. I've never read a student paper like this. I bet you haven't either.

Sometimes you can trap them with individual words. Does she use big words that she can't define when you ask her?

He shook his head. No, she was sly enough to choose a source with simple language. That's why a brochure was so perfect. It's a form of advertising, so the language has to be simple enough for anybody to understand. It's the style, the way it's written that makes me sure she didn't write it. It's just too clean.

He slid the paper across the desk. Kronsky began reading. He was confident: she had to see the cheating. The rhetoric was just so totally unnatural for a student paper. But now Kronsky was shaking her head from side to side.

I just can't see it, Jack. Maybe if I had some of her other writing to look at.

Have you ever seen a student paper that read like that? And another thing: There are no mistakes, not even a run-on sentence or a misplaced comma.

Well, it could always be something she wrote earlier. Maybe she has written brochures professionally. If that's the case, she's not guilty of plagiarism in the classic sense, though you might think about lowering her grade.

Kaiser wanted to say: one of us is crazy, you or me. Was Kronsky really so easy to gull, or was Kaiser a raging paranoid? Had he let his anger toward this student warp his perceptions?

So what if I still go forward with charges?

She can appeal and then the matter will have to be adjudicated by the school. You'll have to prepare a case with samples of the students writing and your comments. It's a time-consuming process, but it's worth it if you really believe you're right.

*   *   *

He raised the issue at the faculty meeting the next week. Had any of the other teachers ever pursued a plagiarism case without the source material in hand? Two said they had, and successfully. But when Kaiser approached them and had them look at the paper, they equivocated. They went further than Kronsky: they said that plagiarism did seem likely. But in their own cases they had been able to trap the student with long words from the text that he or she couldn't define, or in one case, even pronounce. Chatting in the teacher's lounge one day, however, he did find one prof who knew who Veronica was.

With the mouth full of metal? A short girl?

That's her.

She's in the Spanish class I'm taking now. The teacher said she spoke Spanish flawlessly. The girl said she had spent her childhood in Latin America.

So she's a Latina?

Well, I don't know if she's really Hispanic. I think she might be Muslim. One day during Ramadan she came to class with her hair covered in a scarf. When she found out I was an English teacher, she mentioned that she was in your class. And the teacher looked away from him.

Doesn't like it, huh?

The professor shook his head.

Well, she shouldn't, Kaiser said. She's plagiarized on every paper so far, and I think she knows I know.

The other teacher frowned and looked away again, as though Kaiser had suddenly made him uncomfortable. Lord, Kaiser thought, wonder what she's been saying about me? Considering that she's a habitual liar, there was no telling what she might have fabricated.

In subsequent days, he began to notice that when he walked down the corridor where the full-time profs had their quarters, teachers chatting in the hall would suddenly lower their eyes and back hastily into their offices. He was beginning to get a reputation as a department weirdo, for some reason obsessed with this issue, this student.

But there was just no evading it. He was going to have to go forward with the charges. How could he demand anything of the other students in the class when he was letting her get away with this? How did he have any right to stand in front of them as a teacher? As long as he didn't bust her, she was forcing him into a kind of complicity; he was implicated in the crime. She was banking on the fact that he didn't have the courage or the will to go after her, or else had something so bad in his own history that he couldn't afford to point a finger, knowing that the accuser would himself be subjected to scrutiny. Don't make trouble for me and I won't make trouble for you: that was the deal she was offering him.

But it came down to the question of justice, not for him, but for the other members of the class. That's all he wanted: Justice.

*   *   *

You haven't located the source material?

Kaiser was, for the first time in his teaching career, sitting in the campus Disciplinarian's office, trying to bring a student up on charges.

No. But I have copies of her writing both in and out of class. It's clear to me that she's been cheating.

It's always better if you have the goods in hand, said Dr. Cardona, the Disciplinarian. She was a dark-haired Latina in a tan blouse and brown skirt.

You can still bring charges, she said. But it's going to be your word against hers.

I can live with that. I just can't let this go on any further. I can't stand up in front of the class anymore; I'm ashamed to face them.

She gave him a form with two copies attached. It was headed Report of Academic Dishonesty.

You must show this to her and get her to sign it. Tell her that her signature doesn't mean that she accepts the charges, only that she has been informed of them.

Then what?

You also have the option of giving her a failing grade.

Got to be an F, said Kaiser. She's plagiarized at some point on every out-of-class paper that we've had.

You have that option, said Dr. Cardona.

I bet this is happening in some of her other classes, Kaiser said. It would be nice to get corroboration. May I inform some of the teachers with whom she's enrolled this semester?

I don't see why not, said the counselor. The student will have ten days from the day you show her the letter in which to file an appeal.

She'll appeal, said Kaiser. No question about that. What happens then?

The charges will have to be adjudicated. It's out of our hands.

So in whose hands is it?

It goes to Academic Affairs.

Academic Affairs? Kaiser had never heard of it before.

That's the office that investigates these matters. It's kind of like Internal Affairs in the Police Department.

Kaiser had heard of Internal Affairs before. It was usually good for a subplot on the cop dramas rerun incessantly on late night cable TV.

He asked her, But cops all hate Internal Affairs, don't they? I mean don't they feel that it's motivated by politics, and usually goes against the policeman?

The counselor merely nodded her head as if to say, you've got it precisely.

*   *   *

The next day he arrived early for Comp class. Veronica was there as usual, poised and waiting. Well, today she was going to get a surprise.

The lesson for today was Richard Rodriguez's controversial essay which took a stance against bilingual education. As usual, Veronica tried to commandeer the discussion with a speech about how everyone's ethnicity had to be respected. It was as if she were already running for office.

Yes, that's right, Veronica. Rodriguez doesn't disagree with that. But that's not his point. Now if we can move on—

I don't see what's wrong with what I said.

Oh boy,was she going to get it. Right there was when Kaiser realized that this had become personal. He hadn't seen it before now, because nothing like it had ever happened to him before. He'd occasionally had students who hadn't liked him, even hated him, but it had never gotten to this level because the students were so transparently naïve. Kaiser had been made a stand-in for things these students didn't understand and feared in life. You have to know something in order to truly hate it, and they didn't know him. But this was different. He had the notion that it was definitely him she hated, the real, essential him, which she had miraculously intuited without his having consciously revealed it.

Veronica, that reminds me. I need to speak to you for a few minutes after class. He said that very coldly, ominously. It had the effect of shutting her up for the rest of the period. When the class ended and the room emptied, she stood before his desk.

Veronica, he said, as near as I can tell you've plagiarized almost every word you've ever written in this class. She backed away from him. She hunched her shoulders slightly and showed him her clenched teeth, gleaming in their metal prison. She was a trapped animal; a weasel or a vicious little ferret.

I have never been so insulted, she said.

He couldn't believe she had said those words. Real people didn't say things like that; it was a movie line. Margaret Dumont in Marx Brothers pictures said things like that. You even plagiarized those words, he wanted to say, but she went on.

I've had a hard life. I'm an immigrant, you know. This isn't my native country. I'm an underage student. I have to work a full-time job. *I was abused by my own father* (She was looking at him as though he were the evil patriarch himself) and this is the worst, she went on. The worst thing to happen to me yet.

For a moment, the disclosure about her father stunned him into an instinctive compassion, but he quickly realized what he was hearing: Not *I'm innocent*, but rather: *Here's how I justify cheating.*

A lot of people here have had hard lives, Kaiser said, but they don't plagiarize.

And then it occurred to him that she might be still be lying about her father, about herself. He thought: this is a self-pitying person, capable of anything.

I'm giving you an F in the course, Kaiser said. You have the right to appeal. But you have to sign this form. It's not an admission of guilt; it only acknowledges that I informed you of the situation.

She signed the paper, but she was looking straight at Kaiser the whole time.

V

Is this really as accurate as a blood test? Kaiser asked.

A blood test is 99.9 per cent accurate, said the gray-haired little woman on the other side of the desk. She tilted her head in order to look at him over the top of her half-spectacles. This is 99.7 accurate, so there's very little difference.

Kaiser fell silent. It was too difficult to talk with the swab in his mouth. After a bit, the gray-haired woman extended her hand.

OK, that's fine.

Kaiser extracted the swab and handed it to the woman, who inserted it into an envelope and placed it in the desk drawer. The woman explained that she was a retired physician, working as a volunteer at the college health service HIV project. Did Kaiser mind if she asked a few questions?

No problem.

When was the last time you were tested?

Twelve years ago.

That's quite a while.

I haven't been active until recently, Kaiser said.

How often do you use a condom when having sex never, usually or always?

Always.

And with oral sex?

Always.

How many women have you had intercourse with in the last year?

Umm—six.

Was any of these women a prostitute?

Must we use that word?

I'll take that as a Yes. She made a mark on her paper.

All right, she said. Come back in a week and get your results.

She handed Kaiser a ticket with only a number on it.

To preserve your anonymity, she said.

Kaiser had had the test done here at school instead of through his HMO for that reason: anonymity. An attorney on a talk show had said that you didn't want any HIV test, even a negative one, on your records. Even though it showed you were clean, it indicated that you were *concerned.* Insurance companies didn't like to see that.

As he left, Kaiser was pleased to see that no one was in the waiting room at Student Health, just as had been the case when he came in. He had purposely scheduled the meeting late in the day to make sure he didn't run into any of his students waiting for the same outside. If one of his own students had seen him waiting for the HIV test, they might get the idea that Kaiser was gay. Or straight. Or bi—whatever. He found it professionally useful for the students not to think of him as a sexually active being at all.

* * *

When he walked into his Comp class a couple of minutes early as usual, he was surprised to see Veronica Tafuliya sitting in her usual seat. He motioned with his finger for her to come speak to him.

Why are you here?

I'm appealing your dishonesty accusation.

I expected that. Why are you here?

I asked the people in Academic Affairs if I could stay in the class during the appeal, and they said yes. I have the right. See, if I win my appeal, I want to get credit for the course. I'm going to keep coming to class and do all the papers.

This was something Kaiser hadn't foreseen. When Veronica returned to her seat, she flashed him a metal smile, shiny with triumph.

Something had changed, though. She didn't interrupt the class to speak as she had done before. Instead, she whispered to the students on either side of her, giggled and made jokes. He got angry once and snapped at her, but he quickly realized that she was baiting him in order to get him to lose his cool and commit some breach of faculty conduct that she could use against him.

*   *   *

Academic Affairs was located in an office building a few blocks away from campus. It looked like the offices of an insurance company or a law firm, not part of the college at all, and this made Kaiser a bit uneasy. Inside, he introduced himself to Dean James, a stout African-American woman of about his own age dressed in a business suit—unusually formal for a community college administrator.

I'm sorry, Dean James said. The rules say that she can stay if she wishes.

But it's disruptive.

She has the right. You don't have to grade her work. Just collect it. If her appeal is upheld, you must read it and assign a final grade.

Which she could also then appeal.

Of course. She'd be within her rights.

What must I do?

We need copies of the documents you claim she plagiarized, as well as the ones you feel are authentic. Then we need a letter from you describing your conclusions.

With examples drawn from the work. Just like I tell my Comp students.

*   *   *

Veronica Tafuliya was always in attendance, just as she had been before he had confronted her. But now there was a new element. She was tape recording his remarks on a little box she brought to class every day. He didn't want to allow it, but she had referred him to Academic Affairs.

She has the right, they told him when he complained. She has the right.

*   *   *

He didn't know how many in the class knew what was going on, but he felt as if he was going on trial every time he stood before them. She was the one who was supposed to be on trial, but everything had flip-flopped somehow. A dozen times a day, he cursed Academic Affairs.

He was exhausted and relieved when the last day of class arrived. He was going to talk about the final exam to be given the next week, wish the students well and let them go early. It only remained to wrap up one essay that had not been discussed: a family memoir by a Puerto Rican writer who recalled the contrast between her origins on the island and life in New York City.

Her dad wants his family to assimilate to American life, a student said, but he still wants the women in the family to maintain their traditional female roles.

And only those roles, Kaiser said. You're right, Lucia. It's a contradiction that brings a great deal of suffering upon the family.

Someone expressed curiosity about Puerto Rico and its status relative to the US. The last class was a good day for digression, so they went on for a while about Puerto Rico and the question of its sovereignty; how there were groups who wanted to keep the status quo, others who wanted US statehood and a third group that wanted to be an independent nation.

The nationalists are very far left, said a student who was studying the country in his history class. They are admirers of Cuba.

And that led some other students to ask Kaiser about Cuba: he'd mentioned that he'd been a few times, but hadn't had the occasion to go into detail before. Today was the appropriate time, he figured, so he launched into a generally favorable picture of life in the country. He knew he was coming across less ambivalent than he actually felt, but that was OK: he felt that he owed Cuba something. He wanted the students to come away knowing how evil the embargo was, and how it harmed the innocent.

He even hinted about the girls.

The clubs are great, he said. The music is wonderful. And the people are very friendly. That's all I'm going to say about that.

Some people laughed.

But what about their human rights record? It was Veronica, of course.

I'm not entirely comfortable with that term, human rights. It has come to mean only political rights. In Cuba, they don't have certain rights, but they have certain other things more important, like universal medical care, which we don't get. Everything in this country is my rights, my rights, my rights! I'm sick of hearing it! Having rights is not the same thing as justice. That's all I want—justice! Justice!

The students were beginning to give him funny looks. Veronica smiled. He realized he wasn't talking about Cuba anymore. It was time to change the subject.

That's why the American election was so indecisive, he said; real issues were avoided. Then he went on to say that in his opinion, the Democrats should have thrown Clinton to the dogs when he lied. Gore would have become President and won reelection easily.

I think President Clinton has done a wonderful job, said Veronica.

He knew what he did next was going a bit far, but he simply couldn't deny himself.

Well, that makes lot of sense, Veronica, he said slowly, and he turned to erase something on the blackboard, so that he would not be looking at her.

He continued: But I will say one thing for him. With all the lies he's told, no one as far as I know no one has ever accused him of plagiarism.

*   *   *

In Films and Feminism class, he wound up the semester with Luis Bunuel's *Tristana*.

Does Don Lope deserve what he gets? Yes, Berthe.

Absolutely. I mean this young girl is entrusted to his care and then he rapes her. He ruins her life.

Yes, Kaiser said, Tristana's loss of her left leg gives a physical embodiment to the injury he's done to her. Don Lope is essentially her adoptive father: he rapes his own daughter. He has betrayed the most elemental trust that his society places in males. She is no longer marriageable. An even greater injury is the psychological wound she has suffered. Then she loses her leg. The scene where she opens her robe and shows herself naked to the peasant boy is meant to be her statement of rage toward men in general. The fact that Tristana is played by Catherine Deneuve at her most beautiful only makes the scene more horrific. And what about Don Lope shmoozing with the priests there at the end? Yes, Rodrigo, what's going on?

He's become just like them.

In what way?

He was supposed to be a radical when he was younger, and opposed to the church.

Exactly. This was a man who years before claimed to be a freethinker, opposed to religion and tradition, with all kinds of progressive ideas, such as the equality of women. Now he's sipping wine and joking with priests. It's an Old Boys' Club, and Don Lope's a member. I think Bunuel is implying that he always was.

*   *   *

Kaiser showed up at Student Health to get his HIV test results as soon as the required week had passed. He was a little surprised when he arrived at the office, which last week had been bustling with activity—it was flu season, after all. But the waiting room was empty, and only a single nurse sat behind the long front desk. Quiet as a tomb, Kaiser thought.

Hi. I came to get my test results from last week.

The nurse nodded slowly. The doctor's gone, she said. She only worked half a day today. We're on a reduced schedule for the holidays.

But the semester's not over.

Yes, but we always scale down from the final exam period until school starts up again.

When will that be?

First Wednesday of the winter semester.

You mean I'm going to have to wait a month to get my results?

I'm afraid so.

Ha! That's great. Merry Christmas.

You too.

He walked slowly across the quad, leaden-limbed. What a great holiday this was going to be.

*   *   *

The last final exam Kaiser was scheduled to give was the Comp course. Never had Kaiser been so happy to see a semester end.

On the way to the classroom, he stopped by his mailbox. There was a letter from Academic Affairs. He assumed it was a follow-up on the plagiarism case.

The letter was indeed from Dean James, head of Academic Affairs. He flipped it open, but it was not what he'd expected at all:

This is to inform you that sexual harassment charges have been brought against you by a student in your class, Veronica Tafuliya, student ID #61712. This notice will be entered into your permanent file here at Bay City College.

He saw again her face in that trapped-animal grimace as she told how her father had molested her. He still had half an hour before class, so he quickly drove down the street to the office of Academic Affairs. When he walked in, he was greeted by a secretary with reindeer bells around her neck for the holiday. She informed him that the dean was in. Dean James had on a red Santa cap, but was as somber as before.

What's this about? Kaiser asked, showing her the letter. What am I being accused of?

It's a form letter. She doesn't have to specify. You may not be aware of it, but according to college rules, many things can be construed as sexual harassment. Using profanity in class. Or telling dirty jokes.

But I don't use profanity or tell dirty jokes in class.

It could also be a charge that attempts were made to extort sexual favors in return for grades.

I don't do that either. Look, you know I brought plagiarism charges against his same student two weeks ago. All of a sudden, she comes up with a harassment charge against me? Isn't it obvious what's going on here?

She may wish to contend that you made the plagiarism charge after she rebuffed your advances, anticipating that she might bring charges against you. That's the way these cases often go.

Has she presented any evidence to you?

A student doesn't need evidence to make the charge. Any student has that right.

Well, I'm going to appeal.

There's no appeal.

What do you mean?

There's nothing to appeal. It's only a charge. You aren't going to be censured in any way as of now. The letter just stays on file here in our office.

I don't understand. She got to appeal. Why don't I get to appeal?

Students have the right to appeal when their grade in the course is affected. You don't need to appeal because no action is being taken against you. An allegation has been made, that's all.

So is there some kind of investigation now? To ask her to prove the allegation?

The student didn't request an investigation.

But I don't have any way to confront these charges. And you said, the letter would stay in my file here. If I was ever to apply for another job, that letter would be part of the record.

Right.

* * *

Kaiser couldn't really say he was surprised by the sex charge. A sex harassment claim had been a concern of his for years, ever since such cases had come into fashion, because he realized the vulnerability of a teacher—any teacher—to such a tactic. This was another reason why he had been so meticulous about never even making his own sexual preference clear. Or at least he thought he'd been meticulous.

He likewise had never demonstrated anything that could be construed as sexual interest in any student. Any meeting he suggested outside of class had to take place on campus, in a place where there were plenty of other people, such as the cafeteria or teacher's lounge. If he was interested in a female student, his policy was to wait until the semester was over and the final grades delivered before risking so much as a phone call. Even this had happened only a couple of times, and had led to nothing, a result about which he had been secretly relieved.

But he knew now this journey was going to be longer and more grueling than he had initially thought. He usually felt a pleasant sense of closure at final exams, but not today. Veronica was there in her usual seat, of course. Academic Affairs had instructed her to do all assignments and exams while her appeal was pending. When she finished and handed in her blue book, he motioned her out in the hall.

OK. What's this all about?

You shouldn't have to ask.

What'd I do? What are you accusing me of?

You implied certain things.

Like what?

You know.

I don't; so help me, please.

I've been advised not to give you any more details.

That sounded ominous. Was it the school who advised or had she consulted someone outside?

When did I ever show a sexual interest in you?

I can't say any more.

I've never been charged with anything like this before, you know. Do you think anyone will believe the charge of a plagiarist? But the main reason . . .

He paused, knowing in some corner of his being that he was about to purchase a one-way ticket to hell, but as had been the case throughout this awful business, he was unable to stop himself.

The main reason no one will ever believe I would harass you is that . . . is that you're so fuckin' UGLY!!

Now he had said it. He had crossed the line; now it had become personal for both of them. And in his mind he felt that she was speaking for all those women he'd been with south of the border and in Cuba—she was showing him all the anger, boredom and contempt that he suspected those girls secretly felt towards him, but which they suppressed, hid behind a surface cheerfulness as people must do in order to close a deal. Veronica somehow sensed that he had something to hide; in her eyes, frozen in unlinking rage, he could see that she was the representative of those women, their surrogate; the mask was off.

And as bad things were, Kaiser saw a chance to make them even worse.

Tell your Dad, he said, tell him that he has *lousy taste in women*!

Veronica made a little peep-noise and ran off down the hall. Kaiser smiled, but it was not the smile of victory, but more like the unsuppressable shamefaced smile that cops have noted on the faces of handcuffed criminals on the way to jail.

VI

Kaiser wasn't very cheerful during the holidays. After the reading of term papers and exams, and the submission of final grades to the office, he usually had a week or so of vacation to look forward to. Maybe a trip to Tijuana. Not this year, though. He was going to have to spend his free time preparing the case against Veronica Tafuliya.

Busting a student was not something he would have looked forward to under any circumstances, but now he had the additional burden of knowing that he was in a dogfight for his professional life due to her counter-charges. He was ashamed that he had resorted to the crack about her father, but he wasn't sure if, given the same situation, he would have been able to resist saying it again.

He was less ashamed after he read her final exam. He thought it seemed a bit more polished than her midterm. Then came the unmasking: the students had been asked to select four essays out of the thirty or so that had been covered in class. One of the ones Veronica had picked, a personal memoir by Ralph Ellison, was an essay that the class usually covered, but this semester had not been assigned.

She had obtained a copy of an old exam from a former student, and brought a pre-written test to class. She'd filled up the two hours of test time scribbling nothing, and then handed in not the blue book she'd written in, but another pre-done one she'd brought in with her, and made the switch as he was collecting the papers. He could now see that the essay didn't fit the exam question, which was a new one he'd never asked before. That's why, even though it was well-written, the essay would ordinarily receive no more than a B. This essay, however, was going to receive an F.

Now he was so steamed that he didn't even regret the remark about her dad. She was clearly a pathological liar. What reason was there not to think the dad story just one more lie? A shrink on some Discovery Channel crime-doc a couple of weeks before had said that real victims of parental abuse usually lie by saying that it *didn't* happen.

Then came the matter of her research paper: on gun control. Most students who had tried to pass off a bogus research paper at least wrote the beginning and end themselves, but this wasn't even cobbled together: it was a straight-out lift, along with the works cited.

It was then, with no little pleasure that he bubbled in an F grade for Veronica Tafuliya on his final roster, and took it personally to the Admissions Office. It was only afterward, driving home, that he began to truly see the dimensions of his situation.

He had gotten into a he said/she said with a she who was capable of saying anything, anything at all.

*   *   *

Holiday depression really sunk in when he began to prepare the documentation for the plagiarism charge. He drew up a long letter describing his reasons for believing the papers to be copied: the absence of errors, the institutional tone, the stylistic differences between the in-class essays and the take-home papers.

But if she stuck to her position, he was going to have a very tough case. He simply needed the proverbial smoking gun, and there was none. The case would be adjudicated by someone in (where else) Academic Affairs. That arbiter might well tell him to restore the student's grade. Then he would have to give her an A because the material she copied was well-organized and clear. And it wouldn't exactly help his credibility in disputing the sex charge.

*   *   *

He went to Student Health first thing the first day it reopened. He didn't care if students saw him in the waiting room. Enough was enough.

When his number came up, he found a different counselor waiting for him in the rear room, another elderly woman. This lady, like the first, had a set of questions.

Do you have health insurance?

Yeah. Through the school here.

Have you ever known anyone who was HIV-positive?

Not personally. No.

Are you aware of the services available in the community for HIV treatment and counseling?

No.

You'll find several pamphlets just inside the door when you go out.

Oh shit. He could see where this was headed.

The woman slid the numbered paper toward Kaiser and flipped up the top sheet. Kaiser read the words in capital letters: NEGATIVE.

F-f-f-u-u-u-ck, he exhaled. You had me going there.

We always ask the same questions every time, regardless of the result. You'll get used to it.

If you say so.

So long. Be careful!

Kaiser walked out of the office, disappointed that he didn't feel truly happy. Maybe it was because the future held the prospect of many of these rituals. Relief was the best feeling he could muster.

Even that proved to be short-lived. When he walked across the campus, he passed Veronica Tafuliya, her books for the new semester pressed tight across the breast of her long green coat. She looked away from him and smiled; not the full-out smile with braces exposed and gleaming, but a tight-lipped, haughty, smug smile of triumph. She was going to win and she knew it.

*   *   *

Kaiser made a final attempt to find some evidence on the net. He had previously tried to locate her sources by searching under the subject of the paper: fraternities and sororities, for example. This time it occurred to him that that might be the wrong approach. Instead, he simply typed in Plagiarism Detection.

He felt like an idiot. He was presented with a list of two dozen sites: Cheatcatch.com, Plagnab.com, Wordthief.com and on and on. He decided on one called Nailem.com which offered a free trial with a result within twenty-four hours. He got out the copy he'd made of Veronica Tafuliya's paper on fraternities. He had to retype it himself onto the computer, because he hadn't wanted to alert her by asking for a copy on disk. But it went faster than he would have thought. When he pressed the button to send it to the Nailem service, he felt an immediate sense of exultation. Wasn't he getting ahead of things here? No, he just had a feeling about this one. He went down to the Third Street Deli, and celebrated with short ribs, preceded by a cold martini.

The next day he was thankful that he had classes to teach. Anything to keep his mind occupied until seven, when that twenty-four hour period would expire. He even made himself wait two hours past the deadline before he dialed up Nailem. It was a kind of mental discipline to protect himself against possible disappointment.

He didn't realize how good the news was at first. There was a color-coding that confused him momentarily. But he eventually realized that Nailem had located fifty percent of Veronica's paper copied verbatim from other sources. Incredible, because these sources were not Newsweek or the New York Times, but things like the web site for the Panhellenic Council at Kansas State and the student newspaper at the U. of Central Arkansas—even there the relentless Nailem had pursued, and ferreted out. Each of the sources was given a distinctive color, and every time that source was used, the lines showed that color on the paper. Veronica's paper was now a rainbow.

Like in that Elizabeth Bishop poem about catching a fish that he taught in Intro to Lit: Rainbow! Rainbow! Everywhere was victory. Justice! Justice!

Now that it was almost over, he realized what an ordeal he'd been going through for the past few weeks, sensing that the people in his own department were unsure of his credibility. He would be vindicated. The sex charge would, of course, evaporate. He resolved not to gloat or to be vindictive. He would recommend that Veronica be given an F but allowed to remain in school.

*   *   *

Well, I guess this ties it up nice and pretty with a ribbon, said Kaiser. He was again in the office of Academic Affairs. Dean James was going over the material he had presented to her.

I mean, this is beyond the smoking gun, he said. This is like videotape footage of the gun being fired.

The Dean nodded. This is what we need. This is what we like to have in these cases.

This will also blow off that harassment business, won't it? I mean, you can take that letter out of my file now.

The Dean shook her head. The harassment charge is a separate matter. Somebody could argue that the fact that she's a plagiarist doesn't mean that she couldn't have also been harassed.

But that's ridiculous. I mean, she's clearly a pathological liar.

I realize that, but the school rules say that anybody has the right to file an allegation. It doesn't matter if the student is crazy, retarded, or a criminal. They still can file an allegation. They have the right.

The right. What about my rights? That allegation will remain in my file forever.

Nothing will necessarily come of it. But they have the right to file an allegation, the Dean said again.

Kaiser thought: That's the way they work it here.

But he was in too good a mood to allow it to bother him for more than a few minutes. He had already decided to celebrate with a weekend trip to TJ.

*   *   *

First, though, it was time for a visit from his housekeepers. Things had improved on that front: He now had had a steady pair of cleaners for several months. He even trusted them with his keys.

This team was a man and a woman, both from Guatemala. Like many Guatemalans, they had been converted from Catholicism to evangelical Christianity by missionaries. Their old Ford Falcon had bumper stickers saying CRISTO VENGA, JESUS ES DIOS, and SON LOS DIAS ULTIMOS. They were good workers, too. They always spent a full hour at the house; he knew because sometimes he would arrive early and find them still at work. He particularly liked the way they got his dingy kitchen floor nice and shiny.

VII

Kaiser walked the now-familiar path from his motel to the Zona Norte, past the dance clubs filled with discoing college kids, past the Indian women begging change and down the steep hill from Revolución to the Frontera.

He was energized by his settlement of the Veronica Tafuliya business. He had taken the stone out of his shoe, as movie mobsters were fond of saying. And hadn't even had to whack anybody. An F in a course wasn't so terrible. He'd made a couple himself and he'd survived. Besides, the school had a very forgiving policy: she could make the course up, and the second grade would cancel out the first. As for the dishonesty letter, that wouldn't show up on her permanent record unless she made the mistake of doing it a second time, in which case a suspension would result.

Revitalized, he was ready again for risks and experiments. So he had hit on a buddy, another post-50 male, for a hit of the latest youth elixir: a tablet of Viagra. He'd never had any trouble in producing an erection, but he wanted to see if the fabled magic bullet would have any effect on his problem with condoms.

Trouble was, he was almost too hungry to be horny. The buddy had told him that eating a big meal, especially a greasy one, might reduce the effectiveness of the drug. This meant no tacos de carnitas or lobster until afterward. To be absolutely certain of an empty stomach, he hadn't eaten a bite since breakfast. The spitted pork and oily fried chicken in the street stands of the Zona Norte had never seemed appealing before, but tonight the smells were tauntingly appetizing.

As near as he could tell, the only effect of the Viagra was that he was a bit flushed, with a warm sensation in the upper neck. It wasn't like he'd immediately sprung a zipper-buster. Maybe the stuff was all hype. He'd have to wait until he was tested in a game situation.

And what was it he would always think just about now? Oh yeah. *So it's come to this.* And now it had come to this, that he hadn't even remembered to think *So it's come to this.*

The Frontera was getting a facelift and it was going on even now, during club hours. A guy in white coveralls was up on a ladder, working on a new facade for the club, an awning of curved concrete that extended out over the door like a theater marquee. Inside, Kaiser saw that work was being done in the rear restroom as well. He took a seat in a booth against the far wall so that he could see all the girls. The scene was rendered even more surreal than usual due to the fact that workers wearing white painter's pants and spattered white T-shirts periodically walked back and forth from the club entrance to the restroom, carrying ladders, brushes and buckets. The men never threw a glance at the women, and looked as bored as if they were working at some department store or factory.

Kaiser noticed two women chatting at the left side edge of the bar: a tall fair girl with red-blonde hair and a shorter, dark girl with black curls. They seemed to be friends, or at least friendly, and this fit in perfectly with Kaisers plans for the evening.

Buenas noches, he said to the tall girl, whom he found the more attractive of the two.

Sixty, she said without hesitation. His heart was pumping, and he wondered whether he would have felt light-headed even without the Viagra.

Y por ambos? Cien dollares?

It was a deal. His first double-header. On the way upstairs, the girls introduced themselves: Michelle was the *rubia rosa* and Betty was the *morena* with the curly hair. When he bought the room at the top of the stairs, the gray-mustached manager at the desk asked, *Ambos?* When Kaiser nodded, the man's eyebrows arched just a little as if to say Not bad, gringo. It was the first time Kaiser had been shown this kind of respect here.

In the room, as they began to disrobe, the curly-haired Betty asked why he wanted two girls.

Es un sueño? she asked. *Una fantasia?*

Kaiser was a little surprised to even be asked. He had thought it would be a common request, but apparently not.

Sí. Es un sueño. Una fantasia.

The fantasia began to dissipate, however, as soon as they were all naked. First, he could tell the women had no interest in each other. End of *sueño*

/*fantasia* #1. He didn't want to request they perform acts for which they seemed to have little inclination.

Then the bright lights of the room revealed that Michelle was really quite beautiful, much prettier than she'd looked down in the half-light of the club, and he wished he were here with her alone. The additional presence of Betty would prevent any intimacy from developing. Not that Betty was less than cute herself, but the presence of a third person, rather than provoking some kind of primal thrill, in fact created a sense of strangeness and dislocation. Kaiser felt as though they were having sex on the floor of a crowded train station where passengers walked back and forth, oblivious. End of *sueño/fantasia #2*.

Positioning, too, involved altogether too much forethought as he maneuvered to stay inside one woman while caressing the other. He remembered the Yiddish proverb, With one *tuchas* you can't dance at two weddings, and it occurred to him that the expression might have been a euphemism spawned by the very situation he found himself in now. He felt again as he did on that night in Cuba when his back froze up, that he was in some surreal X-rated episode of *Seinfeld*, because while all this was going on, Betty and Michelle kept up an endless stream of patter with each other, making Girl Talk in Spanish and not even looking at him. What they were talking about he had no idea, except that he was sure it had nothing to do with him and the present situation. Again he thought of those trips downtown when he was a child, walking between his mother and grandmother while they spoke to each other in a secret language that he could not comprehend. He had heard women complain of men who watched ball games while they had sex; now he knew how those women felt. And he remembered how hungry he was, just ravenous, and began to imagine enchiladas suizas and camarones rancheros and chiles rellenos stuffed with Oaxacan white cheese.

As to the effect of the potency pellet, he had had no difficulty in getting a hard-on, but that had never been an issue. The Viagra didn't seem to increase sensitivity, and he found himself with his usual problem. Finally, lying between the women, he tried to finish off in the customary manner, but he couldn't relax enough to make it to the finish line . . . he still felt like he was doing it in the middle of Grand Central at rush hour. Then he had Michelle try, but that didn't work, either. The whole time she was priming the pump, she continued to chat with Betty as though he weren't there. Finally, Kaiser had to fold his cards. It was probably the least erotic sexual experience he'd ever had.

As they all got dressed, he tried to start a conversation.

De dónde eres? Or at least that's what he thought he'd said. They gave him blank looks. His Spanish again. One day he'd have to take another course. Where are you from?

Chiapas, said Betty.

Ah—*Zapatistas*, he said. See, he wasn't a complete idiot.

Y tu? he asked Michelle.

Pueblo, she said.

Ah—*mole poblano*, he said. That made him think about food again. Ravenous as he was, he could just about taste the spicy chocolate sauce that had taken its name from Michelle's city. He didn't even wait to walk the ladies back to the club. As he ran down the stairs, he noticed a new sign in English posted on the overhead beam: DID YOU FORGET SOMETHING?

Outside on the street, he nearly raced back up the hill to Revolución. He was so hungry his belly was actually beginning to ache. He grabbed a seat at Sanborn's counter and ordered a house specialty, cheese enchiladas served flat in a soup bowl with red sauce. He gobbled it up, but when the waiter brought him the check, he realized he was still hungry. So he ordered a plate of pork flautas in green sauce. But he was still only halfway full. Next came carne asada in a red mole, followed by flan and coffee.

Tiene mucho hambre, eh? The waiter asked him. Kaiser had sensed a few minutes before that the guy was smiling at him in bemused awe.

You always eat like this? the waiter inquired.

Whenever I can, Kaiser responded. We don't get Mexican food this good on the other side.

*   *   *

He sat picking his teeth. Well, so much for Viagra. And two-girl party dates. Funny how when he had been young, the problem was how not to come too quickly, condom or no condom. Now he was having the opposite problem, having apparently slipped past a middle period where everything was spot on the money. Gilda Radner was right.

On the way back to his motel, he noticed on the side street a massage parlor called, appropriately, Deja Vu. Why not give it one more try?

The room was nicer than at the Frontera: there were potted plants, posters on the wall and salsa music from a CD player. They let you choose the girl here, unlike at similar joints in the States. She was cute and friendly, if a little on the chubby side. They got on well. He showed her his pocket-sized language translator. She said he seemed like a nice person.

She put lotion on her hands and proceeded to work on him. To his enormous surprise, he found himself ready to come in about thirty seconds, just like when he was seventeen. When it happened, she ran the edge of her thumbnail across the tip of his penis, producing an excruciatingly pleasurable sensation. He felt his brains hit the ceiling. Rainbow! Rainbow! Victory filled up the room.

*   *   *

The next day, he didn't even get irritated when the wait to cross the border was an hour and a half. Later, Kaiser pulled over at his favorite stop on the 405. Time to see if he could begin a new winning streak at the coffee kiosk. But that goal became irrelevant when he saw today's quiz question up on the blackboard: *What is a Tijuana Bible?*

Apparently, his question of some weeks earlier had intrigued the person in charge of the quiz. He didn't even hazard a guess; this would be well worth a buck and a quarter.

A Tijuana Bible, said the green-aproned blonde woman behind the counter, is a pornographic comic book. Also known as an eight-pager. They flourished in the thirties and forties. They frequently starred famous comic strip characters like Popeye and Olive Oyl, Maggie and Jiggs, Dick Tracy, Moon Mullins, and Joe Palooka, all depicted in sexual situations. Others portrayed the sexual antics of celebrities like Mae West, Clark Gable and Cary Grant. Sometimes famous political figures were mocked as well. They were usually sold under the counter at certain places like bars and gas stations; they were illegal as both pornography and copyright infringement, and when real people were portrayed, libelous as well. Say . . . you're the guy who first asked me about it, aren't you? Coffee's on the house.

Kaiser insisted on paying.

One more thing, he asked. Why were they called Tijuana Bibles?

They were reputed to be published in Tijuana or Havana, Cuba. In fact, they were almost certainly produced here in the US.

Projection, Kaiser mulled. Attribute your own peccadillos to another person, another culture. Actually, he was slightly disappointed. He was hoping the Tijuana Bible would turn out to be a new kind of revolutionary manifesto, something like William Blake's Bible of Hell, in which the poet, revealing sexual and political repression to be identical, tried to overturn all the moral assumptions of his time.

When he reached his apartment, his message machine was flashing red with word to that he needed to call Dean James first thing Monday morning. Undoubtedly she was going to tell him that Veronica Tafuliya, faced with the goods, had capitulated. He slept well.

*   *   *

I guess it's all over, he said to the Dean.

The by-now-familiar voice on the phone said Not exactly . . .

What do you mean?

She says the paper isn't hers.

What do you mean it isn't hers? That's her name at the top isn't it?

She says that it's not the same paper she wrote.

Well, who wrote it then?

She says you wrote it.

I wrote it?

But the picture was starting to form in his mind now. It was a brilliant ploy; brilliant in its unadorned moronic obviousness.

She says, the Dean went on, that she wrote a different paper, and that you wrote this one in order to frame her. She says you were blackmailing her, that you threatened her with it.

I see, said the blind man. He had underestimated her once again, underestimated her capacity for brazen, open-faced lying.

So what happens next?

We might want you to come in for an interview.

Want me to take a polygraph?

No.

That was just as well, Kaiser thought. Veronica could probably pass a polygraph. She was genuinely convinced the truth was whatever she wanted it to be. That was what she thought it meant to be an American. Maybe she was right.

So it wasn't over. It still wasn't over.

VIII

The next move, Kaiser knew, had better be his. He remembered something that Dean James had told him: it was all right to contact other teachers. That's what he needed: corroboration. It just wasn't possible that he was the only teacher on whom she would try to pull this crap. He went to the main office and found out what other classes she had taken this semester. Most teachers would still have any final exam or term paper that she had written at the end of the course; it behooved an instructor to hold on to those materials for several weeks in case a student questioned his or her final grade. She had taken a full load: five courses. He got the name of each teacher; then he went home and wrote a letter:

> *Dear Professor,*
>
> *This is to inform you that I have just brought plagiarism charges against a student in your class, Veronica Tafuliya. Submission of one of her papers to an internet anti-plagiarism site, Nailem.com revealed that over half of the text had been copied verbatim from other sources. If you have any suspicions about any work done in your class, you might wish to utilize this service, Nailem.com, with which I am not associated in any way. Feel free to contact me if you have questions.*
>
> *Respectfully,*
> *Jack Kaiser, English Instructor*

If he could get one more teacher with the same kind of evidence, then surely Veronica's whole case would evaporate. What could she do; bring a second harassment case against the other teacher?

And why not, Kaiser realized suddenly. There was no limit to what she was capable of; he'd certainly learned that.

Still, he needed every bit of support he could marshal. He didn't know any of the other teachers, so it would be difficult to claim there was collusion. He got the e-mail address of each prof, and one after another, he fired his darts.

*   *   *

The next morning he was awakened by the phone ringing. He knew it was too early for telemarketers, so he wasn't totally shocked when he heard the voice of his department head, Lucy Kronsky, on the other end of the line.

Jack, you're about to get us all in some deep doo-doo.

Is this about that note I sent?

I've had calls from every department. Some of the teachers are really steamed. The secretary from Astronomy came over and chewed me out personally. You're violating the student's right to privacy.

There's that word again, he wanted to say. Rights, rights, rights—what about justice?

Instead, he only said, I thought Academic Affairs told me that it was the standard thing done in these cases.

That's not what Dean James just said. She called too, and she's really on the warpath.

I misunderstood, then. I better go have a talk with her.

I'll talk to all the teachers you contacted and try to contain this, Kronsky said. I'll tell them you thought it was part of the official procedure. I think we can smooth this thing over, but for heaven's sake, be careful in the future. I'm trying to protect you from a possible lawsuit.

He realized he'd been expecting to hear that word *lawsuit* for a long, long time; ever since this whole mess got started. The real fear was finally bubbling up from beneath: litigation, and its possible consequences—loss of money and/or career.

How likely is that?

It's happened before, Lucy Kronsky said.

*   *   *

Dean James scorched him with a flash of her eyes when he walked into her office.

I guess I misunderstood Dr. Cardona, Kaiser said.

I guess you did.

I thought she meant that I could contact her other teachers.

She thought you meant you would speak to some of your colleagues in the English department. She had no idea you'd send letters all over campus. The student could claim that you violated her right to confidentiality.

And she will claim it, too, thought Kaiser, if she ever gets wind of what I did.

Does she know about it? he asked.

Not as far as I know. Lucy Kronsky went to bat for you. She said you've always been a reliable instructor and there have been no incidents like this in the past. She spoke to the other professors. And she thinks she can keep it bottled up.

The Dean was still steamed. She hadn't moved her eyes since they'd started talking.

Even though you technically have the right to contact your colleagues, don't try to do our work for us.

Wait a minute. What did you just say?

I said that even though you did have the right to contact other teachers—

She went on talking but Kaiser had heard all he needed to hear. She had used the R word. He had the right—the right! Now he knew why she was so hot. She had undoubtedly checked and found that if litigation came, if Veronica sued on the grounds that her privacy had been violated, it was the school who would have to take the fall on his behalf. He had the right to inform his colleagues—he had the *right*! The school couldn't leave him to twist in the wind. At least not because of the letter.

*   *   *

When he got home, he checked his E-mail for the first time in several days. He had been anticipating something akin to what he found:

Everyone knows. How long did you think you could get away with it? We'll be watching you. Why don't you resign and save yourself a lot of trouble?
Concerned Women on Campus

My mother told me: Always beware of men posturing as feminists.
(Unsigned)

I knew you were a shitty teacher, but I didn't know you were also a
degenerate. Get off campus, you fucking fraud.
(Unsigned)

Degenerate—he hadn't heard that word in years; didn't even think
people used it anymore. Must have been an older student. Then again,
no; perhaps a very young student using words borrowed from parents.
All the messages had come from the school web site and were therefore
untraceable, not that he would have tried to trace them.

There were more like this. They didn't really bother Kaiser very much.
They were like obscene phone calls—the more offensive they were, the less
seriously you took them. In fact, he considered the possibility that Veronica
had written them all. She had certainly proved herself capable, God knows.
The next message, however, was rather more upsetting:

We, the undersigned, are requesting that Mr. Jack Kaiser resign as a teacher
at Bay City College. We don't feel comfortable with such an instructor as a
member of our college community. We also specifically request the cancellation
of his course Film and Feminism in the upcoming semester.

And this one was signed by several different student organizations:
Congress of Latina Women, Islamic Students Association, Campus Caucus
for Choice, League of Women Students. Even the Association of Progressive
Jewish Students had signed on, apparently to distance themselves from
Kaiser and send a message that this teacher, though a Jew, did not represent
other Jews. He wasn't sure which of these groups, if any, shared an ethnic
identity with Veronica Tafuliya—her own ethnicity was as much a mystery
to him as ever.

Student organizations at a two-year commuter school were not
generally very powerful, Kaiser knew, and the most important ones, for
instance the Student Government Association, had not signed on. He
drew additional consolation from the fact that the undersigned groups
were mostly splinter organizations, not even the mainstream groups for
the people they presumed to represent. The Progressive Jewish bunch, for
instance, distinguished themselves by their leftist and pro-Palestinian views
(opinions which were, in fact, pretty close to Kaiser's own). All it took to
get chartered was a few signatures and a statement of purpose, and the
next thing you knew you had an official group, with each of the half-dozen
members an officer of some kind. The irony, of course, was that until now,

Kaiser would have considered these same radical splinter groups a natural constituency of his own in any dispute with the school.

*   *   *

But you can't just cancel me. I haven't been proven guilty of anything.

Lucy Kronsky had just given him the bad news. She said, It's not because we believe you're guilty. We just want to avoid a blow-up while the matter is pending. Didn't you see the article?

What article?

Oh, excuse me, she said. She reached into her desk drawer and pulled out today's edition of the *Bay City Roller*. There was an interview with Sherzade Shahjehan, the leader of a coalition of campus women's organizations, concerning the case.

Shit, Kaiser said aloud. It was the first time he'd seen his name in any campus publication besides the schedule of courses. About halfway through the interview, the student leader promised to disrupt the Film and Feminism class if the school didn't accede to their demands. We'll make it unteachable, she said.

But you're bowing to blackmail, Kaiser said.

Yes, we are, said Kronsky. He appreciated her candor, at least.

Community colleges have to be even more politically sensitive than the four-year schools, she continued. It's only for spring semester. I'll restore it as soon as possible. I'll even put it on the summer schedule, which you know I've never done before.

What about my Comp and Lit courses? Are they going to be ditched too?

They're safe. We just felt the Film and Feminism course specifically might be a bit . . . well, inflammatory under present circumstances. I'll give you another film course for spring so you won't be hurt financially.

By the way, I'm innocent.

We will stand behind you, Jack. We will back you up.

But my course is canceled.

Just postponed. Look at it that way.

But as he left Lucy Kronsky's office, Kaiser for the first time realized the total vulnerability of his position as an adjunct professor. Nothing about his job was guaranteed; everything was piecework. He lived from semester to semester. They didn't have to terminate him, which might be an action subject to litigation. If the school wanted him out, they could simply say they couldn't find any courses for him, or maybe just one instead of the usual three. He liked Kronsky and knew she wouldn't initiate such a ploy on her own, but sometimes the word comes down from on high.

*   *   *

About this time, his housekeeping crew changed again. The Guatemalan couple vanished, and again he was dealing with a different pair every visit. He called Americlean to find out what had happened, and was informed that the woman had become very pregnant, and had gone on leave until after the delivery. He could expect them back in a few weeks.

So the series of replacements started again; a new crew each visit. And the new people never seemed to be as good, particularly when it came to cleaning the floor that the Guatemalans, Sr. and Sra. Mejia, had gotten so shiny. He would just have to wait until they returned.

*   *   *

Kaiser was only teaching one course, Intro to Lit, during the six-week winter mini-semester. It took temerity, utter gall, in his circumstances to stand up in public and presume to teach Kate Chopin's late-nineteenth century feminist novel *The Awakening*.

So what about Edna? Is she a heroic figure who was going to be defeated by a sexist society no matter what, or did she make mistakes in judgment; mistakes that brought about her own undoing?

I think she made mistakes.

How so, Sun Yee?

Well, she was trying to express herself in all kinds of new ways—as an artist for example, and also in learning how to swim. But it was all tied to this fantasy that she has about this guy Robert. She couldn't let go of that.

That's interesting, isn't it? One of the critical essays in the back of the book talks about that, right? How because women were taught to repress their sexuality as well as to repress the expression of their true selves, it was easy to make the mistake of thinking that the two are identical: that sexual feelings equal the true self. Chopin may be trying to tell us that it's very dangerous to make that mistake. Some women are not as liberated as they think they are.

Some men, either, said a female voice in the back of the room, just loud enough to be audible. A wave of titters swept across through the class.

So they all knew. Teaching at a community college with a fluid student body and no dormitories usually insulated teachers from the gossip mill. But in addition to the article in the student paper, there was now the internet to contend with: undoubtedly the story of his case was in circulation on the student web site.

*   *   *

The next day, a thick brown envelope was in the bin beneath his mailbox. He knew what it was as soon as he saw it there, even before he read the sender's address: Tulsky and McGinnis, Attorneys At Law, even before he opened the envelope and saw the stapled file with the square up in the left hand corner with the identification of the case: V. Tafuliya versus J. Kaiser, Instructor, Bay City College and the city of Bay City, CA.

Kaiser had always had a terror of litigation. He had neither sued or been sued before; his vision of the process was that it was simply a Sisyphean treadmill that drained the life energy of both plaintiff and defendant.

It was mental overload even trying to read the list of charges. He couldn't focus clearly enough to go through the allegations in order; instead, a bunch of fragments jumped off the pages:

> —*that the teacher, J. Kaiser, on or about the first week of November, 2000, did threaten to falsely charge the plaintiff with plagiarism and to give her an F in the course.*
> —*that with this threat the teacher, J. Kaiser, attempted to extort sexual favors from the student*
> —*that the teacher, J. Kaiser, did graphically describe lewd and grotesque sexual acts that he wished the student to perform*
> —*that the teacher created a sexist and threatening classroom environment for the women in the class and for the plaintiff in particular*

Actually, it was the *created a sexist environment* arguments that worried him most. The charges that he propositioned her and threatened her: for these, there would be no witnesses, so it would be his word against hers. But the environment case; that was a matter of interpretation. Now he knew why she'd brought a tape recorder to the last few classes. Everything would depend on how cleverly her lawyers could construe his remarks.

The list of charges was followed by another section announced by the heading, *A Prayer for Relief*. Indeed, thought Kaiser. This turned out to be a list of the reparations. He counted the zeroes beside the sum sought from the school; there were six. The sum sought directly from him alone had only four zeroes, but that would be enough to take every penny he had.

The names Tulsky and McGinnis seemed familiar, and recently so. He remembered the copy of the *Bay City Roller* that Lucy Kronsky had given him; it was still in his book bag. There, conveniently positioned beside the article about the women's organizations who threatened to disrupt his class, was an ad. In the upper right hand corner was a picture of Tulsky, a long-necked guy with a neatly trimmed beard and ponytail. In the opposite corner was McGinnis, a heavy-set dark-haired woman with big black eyeglass frames. In between the photos was a column of copy:

In your educational career, have you ever been:

    -Sexually harassed?
    -Discriminated against due to sex, race or disability?
    -Intimidated by a teacher or administrator?

BE COMPENSATED FOR YOUR PAIN AND SUFFERING!
No recovery, no fee!
We are the best—our attorneys have an excellent record of high recovery.
Free consultation—We can tell you over the phone:

    -How much is my case worth?
    -How long will this take?
    -Will I have to go to court?

Hablamos Espanol
"Impossible is a word found only in the dictionary of fools"—Napoleon
This is America! Dare to dream the impossible dream!
IF WE don't WIN, YOU don't PAY!

Two Guys Who Are Lawyers, Kaiser snorted, remembering an old Saturday Night Live sketch. But he had to admit they were on to something. Tulsky and McGinnis were carving out new frontiers. Lawyers had to fabricate new sources of income, invading and seizing new spaces of social interaction and rendering them litigable. They were the Lewis and Clark of the new century.

*   *   *

You think I deserve this, right?

Kaiser once again required the services of Dr. Phyllis Gluck.

He continued, Even though I'm not guilty of the charges, you think I'm getting what's coming to me.

If you're not guilty of the charges, why would I want to see you punished?

Well, I keep thinking of this movie *A High Wind in Jamaica*. Really quite a good film. Anthony Quinn and James Coburn play a couple of pirates, real cutthroat bastards. Rapists, murderers and thieves. At the end they get sentenced to death, but for a crime they didn't commit—in fact, it came as a result of helping some children, the only good deed they've ever done. James Coburn is incredulous. I don't want to die innocent! he yells at Quinn as they drag him out of the courtroom in chains. Quinn thinks all this is funny as hell. Man, he says, surely you must be guilty of *something*!

That's how I think you feel, Kaiser went on. I'm not guilty of the charges but I'm guilty of something. I'm sure that's what this student thinks. That's how she rationalizes it. He's guilty of something, because all men are like her father. That's how you feel too, isn't it?

What do I think you're guilty of?

Do you shrinks take a special course in being disingenuous? Tijuana. Cuba. I told you all about it. You think I'm a hypocrite. That's what you think. Isn't it?

It's not so important what I think. Do you think you're a hypocrite?

I'm of two minds about that.

Well, maybe I see you as a divided person. That's different than a hypocrite.

Yeah, but are you divided in your judgment of me? I bet not. Level with me.

I'll level with you. I think you have problems feeling and expressing aggression towards a woman.

Is that a bad thing? Shouldn't men be less aggressive towards women?

There are times when a certain amount of aggression is appropriate. She's suing you. You have to respond in kind.

But you'd like to see me lose, wouldn't you? You'd consider that justice.

The flip side of your difficulty with hostility towards women is that you feel they're secretly hostile towards you. So you're continually accusing me of judging you negatively.

That may be true. But you really do want to see me get it in the neck on this one, don't you? Admit it—*don't you?*

IX

Kaiser was contacted by the school's law firm. They would, they said, be representing both him and the school as codefendants. He was informed of the specific attorneys who would be handling the case and what the schedule would be. He should make an appointment as soon as possible to discuss the specifics.

But Kaiser thought it wise to speak to someone else in the field; someone not directly involved in the case. He realized for the first time and to his own amazement that he, though a member of the middle-brahmin class, didn't know a single lawyer in Los Angeles. What's more, none of the people in his circle of acquaintances seemed to be able to recommend anyone.

The best he could do was to phone an old college housemate, Ernie Busker, with whom he hadn't spoken in a decade, and who now resided in Cicero, Illinois. After swapping the usual cordialities he sheepishly explained the true purpose of his call. To his relief, Ernie didn't seem offended. After hearing Kaiser explain the general nature of the case, the attorney had one succinct piece of advice for him:

Get your own lawyer.

But the school is representing me for free.

You'll get what you pay for then. The school's attorney represents the school. Your interests and the interests of the school may coincide or they may not. You need someone to look out for you personally.

Can you recommend someone out here?

There I can't help you. Don't know a soul on the coast.

Kaiser was in a bit of a quandary. He couldn't really go around the department asking other teachers if they knew an attorney who'd ever handled such a case; they already thought he was weird and some probably thought he was guilty. He could, of course, hunt in the yellow pages for his own version of Tulsky and McGinnis, but he'd never found much worthwhile in the yellow pages, and he had no reason to think this time would be different.

A few days later, he was driving south on Lincoln Boulevard when he spied a storefront with *CAFFEINE COURTROOM—Coffee & Counsel* stenciled on the window. Inside, he found an espresso bar with thrift shop furniture, and several bookcases full of legal texts, including a shelf of self-help primers: *Law for the Complete Idiot, Litigation for Dummies,* etc. Best of all, though, was the blackboard with a list of legal services priced from $25 to $35 dollars.

The woman behind the bar advised him that his case sounded like workplace litigation. Those specialists gave consultations from four to six in the afternoons on Wednesdays, which was the next day.

He went over to the coffee house right after his last class Wednesday. The meetings took place on the patio behind the shop, but he had to put his name on a list and wait. Kaiser had a latte and began to leaf through some law books. He found them impenetrable, which did nothing to ease his terror of the process. When he was called out to the patio, a big wide fellow in pin-striped shirt sleeves and aviator glasses rose from his seat.

Bill Feinbein, said the lawyer, extending his hand. A *landsman*, thought Kaiser, somehow relieved. He sat down across the table from Feinbein and briefly explained his case.

This really isn't my line, Feinbein said. But my firm has someone with a lot of experience in this field.

You'll give me a phone number?

Better than that.

He turned around in his chair. At the next table, a woman with her back to him was counseling another walk-in. All Kaiser could see was her long straight dark hair. There was a tennis racket propped against her chair.

Teresa?

The woman turned half around.

When you get a chance, Feinbein said.

Won't be but another minute.

A moment later, the woman turned toward them and stood up.

Teresa Valdevaria, Jack Kaiser, said Feinbein.

Don't get up, said the woman, but Kaiser had already bolted right up out of his seat. Valdevaria had an oval face with big, soulful brown eyes, and she well filled out the UCLA t-shirt and tight black exercise shorts she was wearing.

Jack's a teacher at the community college. He's got a harassment case on his hands. I thought you might be able to help him.

Could be. Let's talk it over.

She reached down and pulled an appointment book out of a bag next to the tennis racket. Kaiser watched the exercise shorts pull even tighter.

Late afternoon is always good for me, Kaiser said. She said she could do four o'clock the next day.

Do you usually represent the plaintiff in a case like this? Kaiser regretted the question immediately. It sounded like he was making a point of her being female.

But she didn't seem perturbed.

I can handle both ends, she said.

Kaiser wanted to make a joke about her choice of words, but he bit his tongue. Hard.

*   *   *

Kaiser was early for his appointment with Teresa Valdevaria, but since her office was in Bay City's popular outdoor mall, he could while the time away with a coffee, or browse the book and record stores.

As he strolled aimlessly, he spotted a sign in the window of Diddy Wah Diddy, the collector's comic book store. It read: *TIJUANA BIBLES*.

Be damned. In the window display was mounted a coffee table-sized hardback whose cover showed a shapely cartoon flapper, a synthesis of Betty Boop and Clara Bow, winking at the reader.

Kaiser bought a copy and went up to Teresa Valdevaria's office, which was on the second floor above a record store. He notified the secretary that he was early and then sat down on one of the big mauve sofas in the waiting room and began reading.

The book reproduced dozens of the old eight-page porn comics. As the coffee-store woman had told him, there were stories featuring classic cartoon characters and movie stars. The standard by-laws of porn were observed: the males had huge dongs and the women were bisexual and ravenous. Olive Oyl fellated Popeye while she was being drilled from the rear by Wimpy. Betty Boop went down on Daisy Mae while Li'l Abner watched, jerking off. Mutt had to bend over like a yogi to go down on Jeff. Homosexuality was a big theme: one titled *Who's a Fairy?* had Cary Grant, so frequently accused of being swish, getting cornholed by Pat OBrien. Clark Gable, on the other hand, was portrayed as all hetero appetite, a characterization probably not far from reality. Same with Mae West on the female side.

Some did not deal with celebrities at all. One, showing a sailors night off in China, depicted pictorially the classic urban folk tale about the positioning of the vagina in Asian women. The artist did deserve some credit for distributing the racial abuse evenly: a few panels later, the Asian girl asks the john *Why all American sailor always want to fuck girl in ass?*

The best ones, though, were the ones that depicted political figures: Stalin, Chang Kai-Shek and Mussolini were revealed as lechers. The artist of a Gandhi strip couldn't spell the name (Gandi) but he knew of the Mahatma's habit of testing his celibacy by sleeping with young virgins, and in this version, Mohandas failed the test. A treatment of the Alger Hiss-Whittaker Chambers story was surprisingly insightful about the role that homosexuality played in the case, much more lucid than had been the newspapers of the era.

About this time, the secretary notified Kaiser that Ms. Valdevaria would see him now. Kaiser stood up and immediately realized that he was about to walk, with a collection of pornographic comic strips under his arm, into the office of the woman whom he was asking to defend him against a sexual harassment charge. Also, the title was *Tijuana Bibles*, and Valdevaria was likely to be a Mexicana.

Shit. If he put the put the book in the plastic bag from Diddy Wah Diddy Comix, at least the title and pictures would be covered up. But he had tossed the bag into the trashcan, where it was underneath several discarded drink cups. He pulled it out, tried to wipe it clean with the palm of his hand, and stuck the book inside. Then he followed the secretary's direction to the open door of Teresa Valdevaria's office.

She stood behind her desk, waiting for him. Naturally, her attention fell on the book.

Reading something good? she asked.

Law for Complete Dummies, Kaiser tried to improvise.

Did they charge you extra for the coffee or was that free?

Kaiser realized that the plastic bag still had wet coffee grounds stuck to it. The lawyer kindly offered him some Kleenex to wipe it dry; then Kaiser shoved it under his chair.

Well, she said, let's have a look at the goods.

Kaiser took the papers out of his cardboard folder. On top was his *curriculum vitae*.

Oh, Valdevaria said. You taught at Eastern.

Yep. Five semesters.

I did the first two semesters of my undergrad there before I transferred to UC Riverside. That's where I graduated; then I went to law school at UCLA.

Really? You might have been there when I was doing grad school in English.

You probably wouldn't remember me. I looked quite a bit different. I wore my hair much shorter and I had huge braces. Completely covered my teeth.

Are you Mexicana?

Salvadoreña. My family moved here in '79. Trying to get away from the civil war.

She began going through the papers in his file. The woman he was dealing with now was nothing like the hottie in tennis togs whom he'd ogled the day before. This woman was all business. She wore little oval reading glasses as she leafed through the material. Outside the window behind her desk, Jack could just get a glimpse over her left shoulder of the distant Pacific horizon, where sky met the blue possibility of the sea.

He found himself wondering if her large breasts were real or enhanced. But maybe such speculations were his way of trying not to be intimidated by this woman, who now seemed very formidable. After a while, she put the papers aside.

Let me lay out for you, she said, the stages that a case like this will go through. The initial stage is called the first pleading. That's where we are now. You have been given notice that the suit has been filed, what the claims are and what is being sought in the way of reparations.

The second stage, assuming no settlement is reached, will be the interrogatories. This young lady's attorney will come back at us with a series of requests for information: they'll want the whole personnel file on you from Bay City College as well as any other institution at which you've taught. They'll also want to know about any non-academic employment you've had, as well as things like the record of any arrests or other civil litigation against you.

Will we be asking the same kinds of questions of her?

You bet we will. We'll want to know her educational history, whether she's ever filed charges like this before, whether she's ever been in trouble.

We'll be doing all this in concert with the lawyers representing the college. Assuming no settlement is reached, we will go to depositions. You and she will be deposed separately, asked a long list of questions similar to those asked in a cross-examination in court. All through the process, settlement offers will be floated by both sides. If no settlement is reached, the final stage is to go to trial.

How likely is that?

Not very. Neither side wants it. It's too much of a crap shoot. Most of the time, settlement is reached long before that point. Pull your chair around next to me and I'll show you examples of what I mean.

Kaiser came around on her right side and leaned over to look at the papers. Her perfume smelled good. She showed him a typical interrogatory filing, drawn from an old case; from the same case, she showed the stenographic record of a deposition.

He noticed that she wore no wedding ring. On the desk was a standup framed photograph of two girls, one who appeared to be around eight or nine years old, and the other about thirteen or so, right at the moment of transition to adulthood.

Are those your daughters? Kaiser asked.

Teresa Valdevaria snapped the picture around so fast that Kaiser could feel the breeze. Now he could only see the black pasteboard backing of the picture.

Let's just keep focused on the business at hand, the lawyer said.

Kaiser didn't say a word.

She relaxed a bit.

Look, you're on the meter here. The more quickly we get through this, the less it's going to cost you.

Just then, Kaiser noticed, in the webbing between her thumb and index finger, a tiny tattoo: three red diamonds in a triangular pattern. He had seen that symbol before, when he had taught in East LA: it was the sign of the East LA Gangster Treys. Teresa Valdevaria had had to climb a very steep slope to get to where she was now.

I'll be good, Kaiser promised.

And he was. They went quickly through the rest of the material, and Kaiser began to pack up his papers.

Of course, he said, worst case scenario: even if I would go to court and lose, the school has to pay my ticket, don't they? I mean, I'm off the hook financially whatever happens, right?

Where did you get that idea? No, not necessarily. The school ordinarily has two simultaneous lines of defense in these kinds of cases: a) He didn't do it and b) If he did do it, we're not responsible.

Kaiser realized that all along he'd been operating upon an unspoken assumption. And a false one.

I guess I just thought . . . I mean, in other cases that I've heard of . . .

The plaintiff usually wants to go after the institution, not the individual; that's true. It's the school, and the state that funds it, who have the deep pockets. But it doesn't always turn out that way.

You mean I could get left holding the bag?

It's a possibility.

No wonder my friend told me to get my own lawyer. Can you work with the school's lawyers, considering that we might at some point become adversaries?

No problem. But it probably won't go that way. Schools generally try to protect teachers from these charges. However, it varies from school to school. I'll need to read your school's policy statements, and the contracts that you signed as a teacher.

One more thing, he said.

He put away the papers and stood up.

You haven't asked me if I was guilty.

That's right, she said, I haven't.

The moment of silence that followed spoke clearly to Kaiser: that's not the way we do things here.

Look, she said finally, we'll have plenty of time to talk about that later. We need to go charge by specific charge, question by question. It's a complicated process.

*   *   *

Kaiser was all the way to the elevator before he realized that he'd left the Tijuana Bible book back in the lawyer's office. He spun around and ran back to the waiting room, only to find the lawyer emerging from the office with the book still in her hands. He was relieved to see that the cover was still hidden by the plastic bag from Diddy Wah Diddy Comix.

Forget something?

Thank you.

He took the bag from her.

But even though the book was in the bag, that didn't mean she hadn't looked at it. Surely she must have looked at it; at least the cover. Who wouldn't do the same? He was asking her to defend him against a sexual harassment charge, and now all she knew about him was that he read pornographic comic books.

When he got back to his car, he hesitated just a second before turning the ignition key. He realized he'd had a certain feeling about her even before he'd left the book in her office. He had this sense from the moment she'd flipped that photograph on her desk around so that the picture was hidden from his inquisitive eyes.

She believes I'm guilty, Kaiser was thinking. My lawyer thinks I'm guilty. Guilty of *something*.

*   *   *

He was reminded of Monica Medrano, a student of his when he taught in East L.A. She wrote so well, as many of the students there did, about her personal experiences. One of her papers described how while living in Texas, she had become pregnant and needed an abortion. The staff at the clinic, all white, had to a person treated her rudely. From the secretaries and nurses on up to the doctor himself, they had let her know she was a piece of Mexican trash who was getting what she deserved.

On the next paper, the students were asked to write about their ideal job. Monica's was to be an accountant. Who in the world daydreams about becoming an accountant? She described in detail the brown tweed suit she would wear to work. She would drive a Japanese car that had been bought new, with that delicious new car smell. She would work in her own office, in a tall building; she would have a desk with a brass nameplate on it, with her own name stamped in the metal. Her coworkers, male and female, would refer to her respectfully as Ms. Medrano. At night, she would go home to her family in her own separate house (which had been paid for in full) in a nice subdivision away from the center of town.

Kaiser was first bemused as he read the paper, but finally it shook him a little. He recalled his own fantasies at Monica Medrano's age: how to get as far away as possible from offices and desks with nameplates. When he saw that gang tattoo on Teresa Valdevaria's finger, he thought again of Monica Medrano and her dream of a life in the orderly sanctum of an accounting firm, far above the depravity of the street. But there was a significant difference. His lawyer hadn't removed herself completely from the depravity of the street: no, as an attorney, she was face to face with it all the time.

*   *   *

He had contrived a way to get his film course back. He simply changed the name from Film and Feminism to Contemporary Cinema and Current Issues. Kronsky had accepted the ruse, though she recognized it as what it was. She felt the elimination of the F-word from the course's title would be enough to soothe feminist groups.

Kaiser wasn't prepared for the result. When he got to the class the first day, he noted that every student on the twenty-five person roster, plus the three-person waiting list, had all shown up. Another dozen students were there unenrolled, hoping there would be an open spot. This was unprecedented, but the biggest surprise was the composition of the class: it was eighty-five percent female. He had never had a ratio like that when he called it Film and Feminism. At first, he was scared: was some kind of femino-terrorist operation being planned against him?

But he soon realized that something rather different was going on. The women were there out of curiosity; they were studying him like a lab specimen. More importantly, they were there to test themselves: were they bold enough to confront the beast in his own—no, not in his lair, in his cage? That's what he felt like: a zoo cat, pacing back and forth behind his bars, while the spectators punctured him with their silent stares. And particularly bothersome was one staring face that he couldn't see: there was a woman in the class, Aisha by name, who wore the black burka of Middle Eastern tradition that covered her completely, head to ankles. Oddly, her feet were left exposed, bare in a pair of cheap flip-flops. That was the only part of her visible besides her hands and eyes.

Originally, he had just planned to teach Film and Feminism under another title, but the name change had actually caused him to realize that he was weary of most of the movies, and he welcomed the opportunity to put together a new syllabus. The first week, he had purposely scheduled Spike Lee's *Do the Right Thing* because of its emphasis on racial rather than sexual politics. The second week, he thought he was on secure ground with Stanley Kubrick's *Dr. Strangelove* until he watched it with the class and remembered how much penis symbolism figured in the film's slapstick. This surprise, plus the hangover from a sleeping pill taken to combat a bout of insomnia the night before, he held accountable for what happened next.

What about all the imagery of the planes and bombs and guns throughout the film? It's all kind of phallic isn't it?

He sensed twenty pairs of female ears perking up simultaneously. This was what they'd been waiting for: Yes, kids, its SHOWTIME!

What is it that causes General Ripper to dispatch the planes in the first place? Yes, there in the back row—

He thinks the Communists are poisoning the water.

And how did he arrive at this conclusion?

He had become sexually impotent.

It was Aisha, the Veiled Lady, who spoke. Odd, Kaiser thought; he had expected a woman in a veil to be reticent to discuss sexual matters.

Some giggles in the room. Kaiser continued.

Right. He's in denial. So Kubrick here is playing off a common male preoccupation: the idea that his sexual performance indicates something very profound about his character—about his soul. Something essential. In fact, what are the words that Ripper uses over and over again?

Purity of essence.

Indeed. But does a man's sexual performance really say something important about him? About his essence? If he had just never really gotten used to condoms, the way they kind of numb the sensation, that shouldn't necessarily mean something about his manhood, should it?

He realized he was looking at two dozen mouths hanging open. He thought: Did I really just say that?

Excuse me, he said. I really need a drink of water.

It was true, too. His mouth had become all chalky.

He ran out to the nearest fountain in the hall and composed himself as he drank. He managed to get through the rest of the class without another incident, but later that day he had to teach his Lit class. The first thing that he noticed when he stepped into the classroom was that Aisha, the Veiled Lady, was in this class, too. He hadn't realized this fact last week at the first class. Maybe she'd been ill that day. But this was strange: he had never had a student in two of his classes simultaneously. The odds against it happening by chance were astronomical.

They were discussing Doctorow's *Lives of the Poets*, and he had gotten to the story *The Foreign Legation*.

Kaiser began. So why does Morgan ask *Did I do this?* After the explosion? He had nothing to do with the bomb that destroyed the legation, did he?

He went on: But you see what's happened, don't you? He's stunned from the blast, getting up off the ground. He's not sure if he's dreaming or awake and we've talked about what he's got bottled up inside: the fantasies about the young schoolgirls, one of whom lived in the legation, fantasies of power and sexual dominance and the guilt about those fantasies and the guilt about his exploitation of the mestizo people in the Latin American country where he gets his museum artifacts and the rage he feels about his isolation and the failure of his marriage, and all that guilt welling up, guilt which he is denying, just like Jack D. Ripper in *Dr. Strangelove* is denying these explosive feelings that keep building up until

BLAM !!!

He wasn't aware how loudly he had yelled until he saw how two guys sleeping in the back row were actually jolted awake. They sat up so quickly that they bounced in their chairs. Again he looked out into the class and saw slack-jawed incredulity from the students. Kaiser continued in a lower voice.

I'm sorry. I got mixed up, didn't I? We watched *Dr. Strangelove* in my film class earlier today. Has anyone here seen it?

Only Aisha raised her hand.

Well, it's a comedy about nuclear war made in the Sixties. But don't worry about it. Anyway, Morgan thinks his own bad thoughts caused the explosion. He wants to be punished. He thinks he deserves it.

I'm losing it, Kaiser thought. I'm really losing it.

*   *   *

It didn't get any better when he got home. He was startled to find that he had received a letter from the US Department of the Treasury. This wasn't about taxes: that would, of course be IRS. It was the Department's Office of Foreign Assets Control. What? Then he remembered where he had heard of that agency before: it was charged with the enforcement of the embargo against Cuba.

He tore the envelope open. Key phrases leapt up at him: *Our office has received information on our 800 line . . . been alleged that you went to Cuba in violation of . . . remind you that travel to Cuba is strictly prohibited . . . need a statement from you . . . please contact as soon as possible.*

The government actually maintained an 800 hotline for people who wanted to inform on people whom they suspected of traveling to Cuba! And someone had dropped a dime on him?

My big mouth, he thought. I should never have talked about it with the class, never. And that had been one of the classes Veronica had taped; he remembered now. Hell, she had probably mailed the cassette to Washington: him going on about how Cubans were very friendly, wink wink, nudge nudge, heh heh.

Well, at least he now had an attorney to deal with such matters. He called Teresa Valdevaria's office and left a message.

X

It looked like the good old days were over.

The Club Frontera now wasn't what it used to be months earlier, when Kaiser had paid his first visits. The wall-to-wall crowds were gone. There was still the core clientele, middle-aged white gringos with long mustaches and longer faces, but there were few tourists, one-shotters, wide-eyed youngsters, lookie-loos or Asian techies. There had been a corresponding drop in the number of ladies available for dates.

All due to the collapse of the tech boom and the corresponding plunge of the share price of Frankencomm. Kaiser realized how much the crowds at the Frontera had reflected the cash spillover from the financial fiesta going on in San Diego in the last year of the millenium, during which a share of Frankencomm had multiplied its value twenty-seven fold.

Bob the Communications Engineer, now the Unemployed Engineer, perfectly reflected the post-apocalyptic gloom. Kaiser had never seen him drink more than two beers, but now there were four empties in front of him, each of which had chased a shot of Herradura Reposado, and another beer bottle in his hand. Even when he wasn't pulling on it, he wouldn't let it go. He had the baleful look of an old hound; his big eyes appeared to push down into the flesh of his cheeks. His friend Rajiv was no longer around; laid off at the same time as Bob, he'd found a spot back in Bangalore. Only Chen still had a gig, and probably not for long: he puffed nervously on his Mild Sevens and spoke of checking out possibilities in HK and Taiwan. Neither he nor Bob had gone upstairs yet. After a time, the Chinese computer ace said that he just wasn't with it tonight and excused himself.

And Kaiser himself was in no mood to cheer anybody up. He'd come down to TJ to try and get the lawsuit off his mind, but this hardly seemed to be the place to do it. He had gotten half-sloshed and was postponing the choice of a girl.

What was he doing here anyway? It was the same experience every time. He thought he was open to having a genuine relationship with one of the girls, but this never seemed to happen. No real intimacy ever developed. He remembered hearing a woman speak who had been part of Andy Warhol's Factory. She said that the artist, in place of an intimacy that he was never able to achieve, substituted repetition. So in the absence of a human connection, he made a silk-screened image of Elvis's face repeated sixteen times and tinted red. And part of his statement was that this was what popular culture provided for people: repetition as a comforting substitute for intimacy. Kaiser speculated that maybe that was why he always found himself back here: for the comforts of repetition. And more repetition.

But something had changed. You could see it in Bob's dour sulk.

Did you manage to save anything up from last year? he asked the Engineer.

Hell, I took company stock, Bob said.

You didn't put anything into cash?

I got about sixty-five K.

Well, shit. Why not move down here? You could get by on that for quite a while.

Bob proceeded in on how you didn't have any rights in Mexico. He was a gun collector, and the government would try to take all his guns away. Without guns, there could be no rights, he went on, and then he moved, with minor variations, into that same old sonata about rights, individualism and freedom, that was so tiresomely played out in the American media.

So why do you come down here if it's such a living hell . . . I mean, to a country that won't let you bring your gun?

Who says I didn't bring a gun?

What the fuck?

Sure enough, Bob hiked up the edge of his Hawaiian shirt just enough for Kaiser to see the square black butt of a nine mm. buried in the pink flab just above Bob's beltline.

Jesus Christ, man, bringing a gun into Mexico? Don't you know if they catch you with that you'll be in prison for years before you even come to trial?

Sometimes if you want rights, you got to take matters into your own hands.

Well, I'm sick of hearing about rights, Kaiser came back at him. The liberals are as bad as the gun nuts like you—worse, even. Everything is rights, rights, rights. But rights aren't the same thing as justice. In order to get justice, sometimes you have to give up some rights. And freedom—Americans love to lecture people about freedom. They love to give people freedom because freedom's free: it doesn't cost money. But there can't be any justice without economic justice. Like in that fucking movie, the one that's supposed to take place here in TJ. You remember the Mexican cop that they use to infiltrate the drug cartel? They ask him what he wants in return, and they have him say a baseball field for the kids. Not a hospital; not a school; not cash money distributed to the poor—a baseball field! That's the old American bullshit: if we just give these poor people our American values, they'll be saved! Like that's really going to help those Indian women begging out there in the street with their kids. Makes me want to puke!

Kaiser realized he had gone on with this tirade longer than he had planned, the same way he had jumped the track in front of his classes a few days earlier. At least this time, he could use the alcohol as an excuse.

Bob had been watching his performance silently, with wide, sullen staring eyes. But when he began to speak, those eyes narrowed in anger.

You make *me* want to puke, Mr. Fuckin' Cheg Weevara! What are you doin' to help that Indian woman in the street? Did you give her a handful of coins before you came in? Is that the economic justice you're talking about? What are you doing here? Do you give these girls a tip when you finish? That make you feel better? Or are you here to start the revolution right in the club? Sure, that must be it! You're recruiting an army for the revolution—a guerrilla army of whores! You're gonna lead an army of Frontera girls back across the border to overthrow the imperialists!

Kaiser had been waiting so long to hear an accusation like this—ever since his first trip to Cuba—that he felt almost relieved as Bob's words cut him to bits. And he actually had a momentary fantasy of himself leading that brigade of Frontera girls, still in their make-up, high heels and club gowns, with shiny Uzis flung over their shoulders. He had on the black beret of Che, and in his hand the new handbook of the revolution: the Tijuana Bible, his own manifesto of liberation from all repression, both political and sexual . . .

Oh shit, Kaiser said, suddenly lowering his eyes. He looked down at the table and put his hands to the sides of his head, resting on his elbows. It wasn't because he was stunned by Bob's rant: he had just seen two of his current students, Leondrick Washington and Mike Aguilar, walking into the Frontera. They were wearing T-shirts and ball caps and they were laughing. He pretended to be drunk as they squeezed past him, in the narrow space between the tables and the bar. They seemed to be pretty loaded, and they apparently didn't notice him, or maybe they were simply incapable of recognizing their prof in a joint like this.

What's the matter? asked Bob.

Kaiser waited until the two kids were behind him before whispering that he would explain another time. Then he was out the door and quickly up the hill, past the legless man who refused to accept money, past the food stands and the clubs churning with the sounds of corridas. He was back on Revolución, stopping momentarily to get a cerveza in a little snack shop, then to his motel room.

There he started burning a Partagas D and drank the beer. What were two of his students doing way down here? Great if word of this got back to campus while the lawsuit was in progress.

Everything Bob had said was true, of course. Kaiser had been glad to hear it said aloud. The deeper he waded into the muck of his desires, the louder he moaned about social justice. As with General Jack D. Ripper, the denial and compensation were too obvious to require analysis. But General Ripper was mad, while Kaiser knew what he was doing: that's the difference between insanity and mere hypocrisy.

But was what he was doing really all that bad? Sure, he went through a bout of anxiety and self-loathing every time he went to the Frontera, but he had all his life felt those same sensations even when he went on an ordinary date. The only way to know the answer, he convinced himself, was through actual experience. That was how you became the *hombre nuevo* that Che Guevara described: by a total immersion in actuality.

I accept the sins that are heaped upon me.

So there he was, an hour later, slouching back toward the Frontera. The students should be gone by now, he figured: youngsters finish quick. Some of the girls in the club didn't like cigars; he flicked his away as he entered.

Good luck—Bob was nowhere in sight. And his students had apparently gone as well. The place was actually getting crowded and beginning to jump a little bit.

Was he crazy or was that indeed his attorney Teresa Valdevaria sitting at the bar in that black dress with the red flower on her left shoulder? He could only see her right side, but it had to be her; same hair, same coloration, everything. He sidled up next to her. She turned to him and smiled.

Sixty, she whispered through the set of silver braces that obscured her teeth.

What had he been thinking? This woman didn't look like his attorney at all; not at all.

He sat down, ordered a drink, and looked around the room again; once, twice, three times. His eyes kept stopping on a tall, athletic dirty blonde. A few minutes later, they went upstairs.

Me llamo Jack.

She said nothing.

Cómo te llamas? he asked.

She still didn't answer. All right, his Spanish was execrable, but he felt she'd understood.

Elena, she finally said, not looking at him.

Dónde vives?

Tijuana, she said, still looking away.

He reconciled himself to the likelihood that there wasn't going to be much conversation tonight. When they got to the room, she flipped off her gray gown. She was big-boned but nicely shaped, and her breasts were certainly real. Any doubts about that were removed when she lay down on the bed and they flattened out instead of standing silicone stiff. She had sprinkled some sort of little shiny sticky stuff over them; he wanted to lick it to see if it was some kind of candy. The problem was that as soon as he got himself into position above her, she jammed her knees up tight under his armpits. He couldn't kiss her; couldn't run his tongue into her ear; couldn't squeeze her boobs even with his arms fully extended.

Qué es esto? he asked. *El sexo por teléfono?*

He rolled over onto his back. But that too was no go.

I don't like the top, she said. He was making progress; it was the first time he'd gotten a complete sentence from her. He could tell she was determined not to interact on any sort of personal level. She was experienced enough to stop just short of showing outright contempt for him.

She got up on all fours.

Doggie, she said.

He went around behind. She should have brought a book to read, he thought as he pumped away. Matter of fact, I should have brought one, too.

Go ahead, she said. You can come in me.

No he couldn't. The condom felt like it was an inch thick. He pulled it off and rolled over on the bed, starting to use his hand. She flopped over on her back and began to play with herself. It was the first remotely erotic thing that had happened all evening.

Afterward, instead of going back to the motel, he went back into the club. He was still restless. A clatch of girls was gathered at the end of the bar gossiping. He had his eye on a brunette with a Louise Brooks bobbed hairdo. She looked a bit like Maria Bartiromo of the financial channel. Why did women on the business channel seem so sexy? Money and sex; sex and money.

The woman saw him looking at her. She came up and put her red handbag down on his table.

Buenas noches, he said. *Me llamo Jack.*

Caridad. You look sad, she said.

Broken heart, he said. I'm trying to get over a bad relationship. I haven't been with a woman since I split with her.

Qué lástima. How long has it been?

He looked at his watch. One hour and seventeen minutes.

She laughed.

Upstairs a few minutes later, Cari peeled down to expose a lovely brown body. Breasts real, definitely. He tried to get his mouth around one.

Hey! No way!

What?

Don't lick me. I don't like nobody to lick me.

You're kidding.

See, some of these guys, they go with three girls a night. They lick somebody's poosey; then they want to lick me.

I haven't licked nobody's poosey. Not tonight.

I don't like nobody to lick me. I fuck and I suck, but that's all.

He sighed. I have to go take a pee.

When he was inside the bathroom, he heard Cari speak.

The girls here they let you lick them?

Sure. On the boobs and the inside of the ear. There's not a hygiene problem. It's not like kissing on the mouth.

Maybe I'm the weird one then. At least you're not like the guy a few minutes ago. A big fat gringo with a ponytail.

Shit. And tattoos?

That's him. He wanted me to lick his *culo*.

Aggh. Did you ?

The other girl did.

Kaiser noticed something at his feet. Poking out from behind the toilet was an object, black and metallic. He reached down and picked up Bob's pistol by the nose. The engineer had hidden it there while he was getting laid, but smashed as he was, must have forgotten it. Fucking gringo asshole, thought Kaiser.

He quickly slipped the gun back in its place. That was all he needed, to get caught with a gun in this place. He would end up spending the rest of his life in a Mexican prison.

Now Cari said it was her turn to pee. While he waited for her, he took off his clothes and lay looking up at the ceiling, mulling over what had happened so far. He'd just been lucky before tonight, he decided. The women he'd been with here in TJ had hidden their feelings, allowed him to kid himself that they were having fun. But the two tonight had allowed the veil to drop away, and he could see clearly what they really thought of him, and it was not pleasant.

Look what I found.

It was Cari, emerging from the bathroom.

Huh? He sat up to see what she meant.

She stood there wearing only black panties, with Bob's pistol held with both hands out in front of her. She was pointing it directly at his head.

And the way she was looking at him—her eyes glinted like an arsonist's. She was indeed ready to be part of a revolutionary army of whores. But he wasn't going to be commander of that army; no, he was instead going to be its first human target. The new revolution would take place over his dead body. Like an idiot, he grabbed a pillow and covered his groin area, as though that would protect him from something.

He was at her whim. She could say the gun was his; that there had been a struggle. This place belonged to *Los Brothers*. They were used to smoothing over situations like this. He would simply disappear, only to turn up in one of those border town mass graves that were frequently excavated on CNN.

Her beach-brown body was tensed, hard and shiny as the pistol in her hand. It was important now to say exactly the *right thing*. Everything depended upon it. But what was the right thing?

He finally spoke.

That's sexy as *hell*.

Apparently that had been the right thing. She smiled and let the gun fall to her side.

XI

It wasn't losing his case that terrified him. He could deal with a loss. The problem was the waiting: the long, slow progress through the stages, not knowing what to expect and more important, when. If there was only a final date set by which everything had to be completed, one could retain one's sanity by counting off the days. It was the open-endedness that was the tormentor.

Yet now that it was actually happening, he was discovering anew the truth of the old bromide about how eventually one became used to anything. It was simply part of his life now, part of his job. He complied with each new request for information and checked in with his lawyer as various settlement offers were floated by both sides.

Their offers haven't really been serious up to this point, Valdevaria said. So ours haven't been either. They ask for a ridiculous sum; we respond by telling them we won't counter-sue or ask for expenses if they slip away quietly. I think you can take it for granted that nothing substantive is going to happen until after depositions.

She did, however, have good news for him on the Cuba situation. She had gone over the regulations from the Department of the Treasury, and it appeared to her that, as an upper-level academic doing non-profit research, he was permitted to travel to Cuba in absolute legality. He could even claim it as a deduction at tax time.

You mean I've actually been in compliance with the law right from the start?

It looks that way. You should have some evidence that you did scholarly research just in case.

I took a photo of Ernest Hemingway's boat.

That will probably do it.

*   *   *

So what does Ginsberg mean by saying he was a communist when he was a kid and he's not sorry? If he's not sorry, why isn't he still a communist? He talks in the poem about all these stirring political rallies his parents took him too when he was a kid, about the Spanish Loyalists and Sacco and Vanzetti and the Scottsboro Boys—don't worry if you didn't recognize these names. They were the great left wing causes of the twenties and thirties. So why is Ginsberg no longer a communist?

No hands went up.

Well, he was gay for one thing, Kaiser said, as you remember from *Howl.* You couldn't be a Communist Party member if you were homosexual. And they certainly didn't want anyone who smoked marijuana and boasted of being psychopathic, as Ginsberg does near the end of the poem. Even though he sympathizes with their goals, he realizes that no strictly ideological movement can really accommodate the complexities of the human personality. Maybe that's why communism failed. And the left wing in this country never really recovered from the sixties, you know, never figured out a way to integrate those old economic concerns with the new issues regarding gender and cultural identity. For instance, Ginsberg visited communist Cuba in the sixties and was thrown out of the country for saying publicly that he had sexual fantasies about Che Guevara.

Some laughter. It was time for class to end.

Well, we'll have to pick it up at this point on Thursday. The assignment is on the board.

The desks creaked and rattled as the students departed. One, however, stopped at Kaiser's desk. It was Rich Goines, who'd taken Kaiser's Comp class a semester before. He was an older student, mid-thirties, who wore a retro Tab Hunter buzz cut and black shorts with Doc Martens, all of which declared him an out gay. Kaiser had been pleased when Goines turned up in the Lit class; not only was Goines a good student, but Kaiser felt that it meant that Kaiser must have handled gay issues pretty well in the previous course.

You've been to Cuba a couple of times, haven't you? he asked Kaiser.

A couple.

Think you might go again sometime?

It's very likely, said Kaiser.

I have a friend who I think would like to talk to you.

What's it about?

I think I'd rather let him tell you.

Kaiser shrugged.

Okay, he said, you know my office hours.

*   *   *

On deposition day, Kaiser was to meet Teresa Valdevaria in her office at eight-thirty AM. Proceedings were scheduled for nine, and she wanted a half an hour to prep him for the event.

When he walked into the waiting room, however, the secretary immediately punched a button and said, He just walked in.

Teresa Valdevaria came out immediately.

They're already here, she said. They claim they had the time wrong.

You think it's some kind of a ploy? Kaiser asked.

Who knows? They can't wait. Anyway, there wasn't that much I needed to say. The main thing is: answer truthfully, but give them as little as possible. The shorter your answer, the better . . . *No; Yes; I don't remember; I don't know*. These are the best answers. Otherwise, little details you give them might seem irrelevant to you, but may turn out to be items they can twist around. Keep in mind that everything you say can be used against you somehow.

She walked into an office where Tulsky, McGinnis and a reporter were already seated. Both of them, thought Kaiser. This case must be pretty important.

This room was not Teresa Valdevaria's office, but a rectangular chamber lined with shelves of law books. The space was dominated by a long mahogany table. He and his lawyer sat on one side, facing Tulsky and McGinnis, with the reporter at the far end. At the center of the table was a stack of papers.

Tulsky was the one who was going to do the questioning. There was the usual preamble about date, place and time and then Kaiser was asked some standard stuff about his name, age, address, education. Then there were questions about employment history; how long he'd been a teacher, which schools. As in the ad Kaiser had seen, Tulsky had a long mustache and a pony tail. He was tall, maybe six and a half feet. When he leaned forward on his elbows to ask questions, he almost head-butted Kaiser.

Q Is this an accurate record of your employment as a teacher?

He showed Kaiser the resume Kaiser had submitted to the court.

A　Yes.
Q　And at any of these teaching jobs have you ever had a grievance filed against you by a student?
A　Not that I know of.
Q　Not that you know of?

Teresa Valdevaria cleared her throat loudly. He got the hint.

A　No. Never. *Jamas.*
Q　You're not married, are you Mr. Kaiser?
A　Noop.
Q　Ever been married?
A　No.
Q　Ever had a long relationship with a woman?
A　Long enough.
Q　Hmm—do you dislike women?

Kaiser whispered in his lawyer's ear, They can't ask this kind of stuff can they? About my prior history? I mean, it's like with the woman who says she was raped, isn't it? You can't bring in her sexual history to damage her credibility.

She answered, In a civil deposition, they've got more leeway than in a criminal trial. I can still make objections and have portions of your testimony ruled inadmissible after this is over. Oh, one more thing I should have told you earlier. You can't take the Fifth. So keep to the brief answers: No, Yes, I don't know.

Tulsky was getting a little flushed. Please advise your client not to interrupt my questions. The reporter will note that the witness and counsel just conferred off the record.

It appeared Tulsky was going to do all the questioning. McGinnis sat beside Tulsky, bent over a pad, taking notes. She handed him a paper with something written on it.

Q　You seemed to imply that you'd never had a long relationship with a woman. Why not?
A　Oh well, that's complicated I suppose there might have been a fear of commitment. And I always enjoyed being alone; the independence of

it. Then again, it probably has roots in my family, early childhood that sort of thing. I was never close to my mother, I suppose . . .

Teresa Valdevaria threw down her pencil on the desk. She leaned towards him and spoke into his ear behind her raised hand:

This is a deposition, for God's sake, not a therapy session! Give them as little as possible!

With her so close, Kaiser could smell her shampoo and the perfumed soap she showered with in the mornings, and he realized that it was her presence that had caused him to open up during the questioning. He was trying to explain himself to her, not Tulsky and McGinnis; to justify himself in her eyes. Tulsky began a new line of questioning.

Q Ever been to Cuba, Mr. Kaiser?
A I . . . Yes.
Q What was your interest in traveling to Cuba?
A Academic research. I'm going to write about Ernest Hemingway.
Q Any other reason?
A That's the main one.

This is entered as Exhibit 1, Tulsky said. He produced a Walkman from his briefcase and placed it on the table. Kaiser knew right away: Veronica's tape of the class. It was all cued up and ready to go. Kaiser heard his own voice talking about Cuba, the music, the clubs and the nightlife, and then saying, The people are *very friendly*, and the class laughing.

Q Is that your voice?
A Yes.
Q What did you mean by that *very friendly*?
A Just what I said.
Q It seemed to get a laugh from the class. Why?
A I don't remember. Maybe someone did something funny.
Q Are you aware that telling jokes or making sexual innuendoes that some
   in the class consider offensive can be construed to be a form of sexual
   harassment by a teacher?
A No. I mean, that wasn't what I was doing.
Q Are you aware that many men go to Cuba for the purpose of sexual
   indulgence?
A I've heard that rumor.

Q   What do you think about this so-called sexual tourism?
A   Well, it reflects a deplorable inequality in wealth between countries. And it can be a form of exploitation.

So far, so good. But Kaiser just couldn't leave well enough alone.

A   But I don't think having sex with a person is the worst thing you can do to them. I think there are far worse forms—

His lawyer kicked him so hard under the table that he thought for a second that his shin might be fractured. And he realized that once again he'd actually been speaking to her.

But now Tulsky jumped to a new track. He slid a paper across the table at Kaiser. Exhibit 2, he said.

Q   Have you ever seen this before?
A   Yes. It's one of Veronica Tafuliya's papers. Or rather, one of the ones she copied from another source.
Q   Will you read aloud what's written at the very end?

Kaiser flipped to the very last page. Above his own writing—a brief note about plagiarism—someone had hand-printed a message:

A   TURKS ARE LIVING PROOF THAT JEWS FUCK CAMELS. Hah!
Q   You find that amusing Mr. Kaiser?

Kaiser couldn't stop chuckling. This had not been one of the original allegations, so he had not been prepared for it.

A   Well, I never heard the joke before.
Q   Really? Didn't you yourself write those words?
A   No. Of course not. I didn't even know Veronica was Turkish. Is she Turkish?
Q   What's important is that you seem to have thought she was Turkish.
A   But I didn't. And I didn't write this. Look, I'm a Jew myself. You could argue that this defames Jews worse than Turks. I mean, you're a Jew; would you want people thinking that you went around fucking camels?

Q I don't recall having ever told you I was Jewish. You seem to be rather quick to make assumptions about a person's ethnicity. On or about the fifteenth of September, did the plaintiff Veronica Tafuliya come to speak to you at your office hours?

A That sounds about right.

Q And what was to be the purpose of that conference?

A She was unhappy with the grade she'd received on a paper. I told her that she was lucky she didn't get an F since she'd attempted to plagiarize on the first draft.

Q And did you imply that you would bring charges against her if you were not granted sexual favors?

A No.

Q Did you imply her grade would be raised to an A if she granted you sexual favors?

A No. Never.

Q At the end of the meeting, did you shake the student's hand?

Ugh. He remembered that clammy little handshake.

A Yes. It was to signify what I hoped was our understanding that she'd do her own work from here on.

Q And as you shook hands, did you not tickle the inside of Veronica Tafuliya's palm with your middle finger?

This too was a new allegation.

A No!

Q Was that not also to signify an understanding?

Object to the form, said Teresa Valdevaria.

What happens now? Kaiser asked.

What happens now is you answer the question, said Tulsky.

But there was an objection, Kaiser responded.

Do you see a judge around? Tulsky said.

I make an objection, explained Valdevaria to her client. It becomes part of the record of the deposition. A judge rules on it before the trial. A lot of this will be tossed out. But answer for the time being.

A All right. The answer to your question is No.

Q Did you on another occasion ask her to bring you a pair of her dirty underwear, telling her, Make sure they're good and stinky?

Objection, said Teresa Valdevaria.

A No! Never!

Q Did you promise to give her an A if she would sit on the front row of class, wearing no panties beneath her skirt, and cross and uncross her legs repeatedly?

Objection.

A Jesus! No!

Q Did you on another occasion pull Veronica Tafuliya aside, telling her you needed to speak to her in confidence; and did you, instead of whispering, lick the inside of her ear?

Objection.
Kaiser suddenly recalled Cari at the Frontera: *Don't lick me! Don't lick me! I fuck and I suck, but that's all!*

A No! My God, did she tell you that?

He knew now that he had again underestimated Veronica, and that the worst by far was yet to come.

Q Did you on another occasion give her an empty Coke bottle, telling her to in your words, Make tee-tee in this and bring it back ?

Objection.

A Of course not!

Q Did you on another occasion pass Veronica Tafuliya in the hallway as she was bending over to drink from a water fountain, and put your hand on her buttocks?

Objection.
He remembered the woman at the Frontera with the sunburst on her back, crouched in front of him for doggy entry.

A   I don't believe this. No, no, no.

Q   Did you on another occasion take a pen out of her hand and put in your pants pocket and tell her that she would have to go look for it?

Objection.

A   Don't be ridiculous! No.

He looked at his attorney and she looked back at him. She showed no emotion. Had she started to believe he was capable of such things? Had she believed it all along?

Q   And when she placed her hand in your pocket, had you cut out the cloth so that she felt your naked erection?

He remembered himself sandwiched in between Betty and Michelle, asking the latter to jerk him off.

Silence. Kaiser's lawyer finally said, Objection.

A   Good God! Where does she come up with this stuff?

Where indeed? Was Veronica's imagination really so fecund, or had she been led along, encouraged to embellish by her attorneys, as had happened to the children in the notorious cases where pre-school teachers had been falsely charged with molesting their students? He realized that Tulsky's partner McGinnis, silent all this time, had stopped taking notes and was looking at him with a cold, fixed rage that he'd only seen once before in his life. When was that? Yes, this was the expression Veronica Tafuliya had worn when she said, *I was even abused by my own father.* Maybe there was a special bond between Veronica and this Christine McGinnis. He now had the sense that McGinnis was the brains of this outfit, and Tulsky merely her ventiloquist's dummy. Tulsky spoke again.

Q   Answer the question.
A   No. It never happened!
Q   And did you on another occasion try to get her to meet you at your home after hours, at which time she was to squat on a glass table in the middle of the room and defecate on the glass, while you lay below the table on the floor, masturbating?

*   *   *

Kaiser was too blitzed after the deposition to do anything except lie on his sofa and look at the ceiling. The phone rang sometime around dinnertime. It was Teresa, calling to reassure him. She apologized for not speaking to him at length after the deposition, but she had had a court date.

Most of what went on today was intimidation, she said.

It worked.

For instance, in child custody cases, it's common for the wife to accuse the husband of molesting the kids as a tactic. It's become almost pro forma. Usually, those charges don't make it into the trial, if the case goes that far.

Some game of liar's poker you people got going.

By her silence, he could tell that he'd hit a nerve.

Well, I suppose you're going to start telling lawyer jokes now, huh? was her response.

Look, do you think they've shown us all their cards? Or could they be holding something back in order to sandbag us in court?

That would be unusual, she said. The goal is to get a good deal without going to trial. It's possible you've seen the worst.

Except I might have to go through it all again in a public courtroom.

If it ever gets that far. Of course, discovery is still going on. New stuff comes up all the time.

Yeah, as fast as Veronica can make it up.

He wanted to ask his lawyer if she could possibly believe any of the accusations, but by now he knew better. That night, unsurprisingly, his insomnia returned. Now it would begin again; the nights of agitation and the painful unreal days.

XII

Have you ever considered asking your lawyer out? Dr. Phyllis Gluck asked Kaiser.

Yeah. Once for about five minutes I considered it.

And?

Come on, doctor. I am literally, as they say, old enough to be her father.

But you've indicated you like young women.

Hah-hah. Very funny.

You seem attracted to her.

So? she's got a whole life ahead of her. And you're forgetting something. I think it's better than fifty-fifty she believes some of these allegations against me are true. I'd ask her point blank, but I know I wouldn't get a straight answer. Just like I know you won't give me one for the same reason. Professionalism.

So you wouldn't necessarily believe her even if she said she didn't believe you were guilty.

Not necessarily, right. Look, the last thing I need right now is to complicate my life. I'm having trouble sleeping. That's why I'm here. I think I need something to help me.

*   *   *

The Nicolas Cage character in *Vampire's Kiss* is what people used to call a lounge lizard. He hallucinates that one of his singles-bar pick-ups has bitten him and turned him into a vampire. It's clear that he is hallucinating, right? That's the difference between this and a traditional horror film. Come to think of it, he might be hallucinating the pick-up as well . . . not likely you'd find Jennifer Beals in a pick-up bar. Well, anyway, this was part of a rash of vampire movies at the start of the nineties. Why do you think this genre experienced a resurgence in popularity then?

There was a moment of silence. Then someone in the last row ventured.

Yes, Orlando.

AIDS?

Good guess. That's one theory. The creator of Dracula, Bram Stoker, died of syphillis. It's like AIDS in the fact that people can be carriers for many years, infecting others without showing any symptons.

I think that there's another level.

Again, Aisha the Veiled Woman was speaking. Kaiser actually dreaded seeing her in class. Completely covered as she was, she became a blank screen onto which he would project his paranoid fantasies. He felt she was always looking straight through him, hidden eyes full of rage.

Yes, Aisha.

Did you notice that the women he picks up, as well as the secretary that he torments at work, all have something in common?

What, besides being female?

They're all women of color. The pick-ups are African-American; the secretary is Puerto Rican.

She was right. Why hadn't Kaiser noticed that?

She continued: He is tormented by guilt because he knows his power is false. He hits on dark women because he suspects they're easy—not like real women, who are white and cold. His power over the women he picks up seems as false as his power over the secretary at work—it's not earned, but something he inherited because of his race. He picks up a dark woman in a club, the next day he tortures his secretary in the hope that she'll strike back and give him the punishment he knows he deserves.

Damn, thought Kaiser, she's good. Then he froze. Was it just that he got only five hours sleep the night before, or was that voice familiar?

And of course, Aisha continued, the dream woman that his psychiatrist fixes him up with in the fantasy is white and blonde—the kind of woman he doesn't feel he deserves.

Was it—Could it possibly be that it was Veronica behind that veil? With a tape recorder in her lap hidden under that black burka? The sleeplessness had distorted things to the point where he couldn't trust his perceptions.

The class was turning into a dialogue between himself and Aisha. The other students were beginning to look at him with a what-about-us-are-we-potted-plants impatience.

And it doesn't work out, even in fantasy, Kaiser said. We can hear Cage doing both voices, arguing back and forth.

Guess you could call him an Undead White Male, Aisha said, and there was a scattering of laughs.

* * *

After the class, he headed for the Admissions Office, where copies of all student photo-IDs were kept. He asked the secretary to look up Kandisha, Aisha and gave her the student's ID number. The secretary pulled out a long drawer and began flipping through the files.

Here, she said. Kaiser's fears were confirmed: the picture showed only a veiled head.

We can't make them remove it, said the secretary. It would infringe on their right of religious expression.

Kaiser had occasionally seen veiled female students on campus in the years that he'd been teaching at Bay City, and he'd wondered how teachers dealt with some of the problems presented by the situation: how could you tell that the woman under the veil taking the test was the same person who was actually enrolled in the class? But his own case was a much thornier problem: suppose the person under the burka was an enemy, a spy hoping to entrap him in some incriminating statement?

* * *

Rich Goines and his friend Ricardo sat across from Kaiser in the Bay City College Teachers Lounge. Ricardo was about the same age as Goines, thirty or so. He wore an *AIDS Walk LA* T-shirt and a baseball cap with the logo Outrage, the name of a famous Santa Monica Boulevard gay bar. On the table before him was a stack of paperbacks.

Rich Goines said, Ricardo has something to ask.

Kaiser said, You're Rich and he's Ricardo?

Goines chuckled. I tell people he's my evil twin. They say everyone has one, you know.

Rich says you go to Cuba frequently, Ricardo said.

Well—not that frequently.

I have a favor to ask of you. I have a friend there who writes. He always asks me to bring him books when I come back for a visit. Books that are unavailable in Cuba for political reasons. The last time I went, I got a full search and they found the books. They didn't arrest me—it's part of their propaganda that they don't ban books—but they informed me that I was now on their list to be searched every time, and if books were found again I would be denied admittance to the country. Not only that, I was pretty sure I was under surveillance while I was there. Actually, I think that's why they let me in: so they could follow me. They wanted to see who I met with. But I had friends who told me how to evade them. And I got a real going-over a week later on my way out of the country. They wanted to make sure I wasn't carrying messages from Cuban dissidents. Anyway, I was just hoping—I mean if you could take them the next time you go.

It means a lot to him, Goines said. I'll try to make it up to you with a gift certificate for the Starbucks where I work.

But what makes you think I'd be any more likely to get them through than you'd be?

You're not Cuban. Returning Cubans always get much tighter scrutiny than tourists.

Indeed, Kaiser had never been searched upon entry. He looked at the books on the table; the authors were Guillermo Cabrera Infante, Reinaldo Arenas, Zoe Valdes—Kaiser had read them all. They constituted a veritable Who's Who of Cuban dissidents in exile. Even worse, the books were in Spanish; Kaiser might be able to talk through English translations as his own reading, but it would take them about five minutes to find out that Kaiser himself couldn't speak Spanish. Then *Who are these for?* would be the next question. Or worse, maybe they wouldn't even ask who the books were for, but put him, like Ricardo, under surveillance, and there would be trouble—not for Kaiser, but for the recipient.

I'm not sure when I'll go next.

Whenever. Just take the books now and keep them until the next time you go.

He handed Kaiser a card with the name Lázaro Perdomo printed on it, with an address on Trocadero Street in Havana and a phone number.

Kaiser was a little irritated at being put in this situation. What right did they have to ask this of him; what right? This wasn't his fight; as matter of a fact, he wasn't even sure what side he was on. Besides, he went to Cuba for vacations, not for such melodrama.

All right, Kaiser said. I'll do it.

*   *   *

When he got home, he found that his lawyer had left a message for him. *Call me. I think I've got some good news for you.* She even left her home phone number, something that she had never done before.

I think you'll be glad to hear, she said when he called, that there's been an offer to settle by the school, and the students attorneys have tentatively accepted. The big thing is that you're part of the deal in return for the cash settlement and the restoration of her original grade in the course, she will drop all charges against the school and against you as an individual. All you have to do is sign some papers acknowledging the settlement and waving the right to future counter-suits and you can put this all behind you.

For weeks Kaiser had fantasized about such a resolution. Anything; anything to get it over with: no more insomniac nights watching the international market report at three AM, and no more confused, paranoid days wondering if his students could tell how close to the edge he was. That's why he was as surprised as his lawyer by what he said next.

I'm not sure I want to settle.

What do you mean? I thought this was exactly what we were hoping for.

If I allow the school to settle in my behalf, it will leave an implication of guilt in a lot of people's minds. I'll still get those funny looks from the other instructors. And it will mean giving her an A in the course. I can't do that.

Look, Jack, you have to be realistic.

Maybe I am being realistic. I'm an adjunct teacher, you know. They don't have to give me courses. They can quietly phase me out if they don't trust me. I need vindication.

In his lawyer's eyes as much as the school's, Kaiser realized.

You have to understand. The school is going to settle regardless. If you don't join, you'll be left hanging. It'll just be you and her.

Yep.

As your attorney, it's my duty to advise you to take the offer. I think you're making a terrible mistake. I've seen your financial statement, Jack. You can't afford to keep this going.

His lawyer was referring to the statement of assets he had been required to fill out as part of the suit.

Veronica can afford it, though, Valdevaria said. They just got a tidy sum in the settlement with the school. If you turn them down, we go to trial and the deposition was just a little taste of what that will be like.

Kaiser paused for a moment remembering that ordeal.

I just can't see any way out. I want justice, that's all. Will you continue to represent me as my attorney?

He heard her take a breath, Yes, she said at last, I don't think it's fair to leave you at this point in the process.

When he hung up the phone, Kaiser sat down and panicked: My God, what did I just do? he said out loud. He looked at the phone for a full five minutes, but in the end he did not pick it up and call his lawyer in order to reverse his decision.

*   *   *

Do you see what she's doing here? When Robert speaks of "the wild dream of your in some way becoming my wife," he's essentially proposing marriage to Edna. This is not an action without courage on Robert's part. Remember, this was over a hundred years ago. In order for this to happen, she will have to divorce Leonce and remarry. There will be a scandal, of course. Even as a married couple, they will not be able to associate with the Ratignolles and the other Creole families. Robert's business prospects will be damaged. Still he's willing to say, *Okay, let's bite the bullet. It will be tough, but we can still make it as long as we become a married couple.* Yet Edna doesn't just reject the deal, she says she finds the offer of conventional marriage laughable. *I give myself where I choose,* she says. What do you think of her decision? Why is she so incapable of compromise?

Because she doesn't want to win. She wants to lose.

It was Aisha speaking.

Explain please, Aisha.

She is self-destructive. This is what she has wanted all along. She really wants death. That is the meaning of that memory image that keeps coming back to her.

You mean the memory of how she got lost in the cornfield as a child and experienced a kind of rapture. But some people still see her as a heroic figure. They would say that her demands are reasonable, and that society is at fault.

No. The flaw is in Edna's character. We must all accept some compromises. That is the way of life. So death is the only way out. She has secretly wanted that all along.

*   *   *

Kaiser's relationship with Americlean was becoming increasingly troubled. He had never found a pair of cleaners as good as Sr. y Sra. Mejia. The two Nicaraguan ladies that he had now didn't take a full hour to clean the house. He knew because he had returned to the apartment after forty minutes during their last visit and found that they had already departed. The place just didn't look as good as when the Mejias were there. The blinds had black smudges around the edges and there were cobwebs in the corners of the ceiling. And his kitchen floor that looked so shiny when the Mejias did it now looked gray and dingy to him.

He was a little indignant. According to the terms set by Americlean, he was entitled to have the cleaners do a laundry load and wash the dishes as well as clean the house. He preferred to do his own laundry and there were never any dishes, since he invariably dined out. The least they could do was to get the floor shiny.

So before the next visit, Kaiser took a little Pepto-Bismol and dropped a tiny pink spot right in the center of the kitchen floor, just large enough to see with the naked eye. A half-hour later, the Nicaraguans arrived: a stout older lady in an apron, her gray hair pulled into a bun, and a younger girl with long hair, blue jeans and a man's blue work shirt with the tail out. He departed as he usually did at this point in the process to run whatever errands were necessary for the day. He returned after thirty-five minutes.

Has the kitchen floor been cleaned?

Sure, said the younger woman, the one who spoke English.

He had them now.

No, it hasn't. Not well. Look.

He pointed at the pink spot on the floor.

See that.

The younger woman sighed. I'll go over it again, she said. A minute later she was on her knees with bucket and sponge.

Kaiser immediately felt an unpleasant twinge. He sat down in his big rattan chair and looked around the apartment. Really, it looked okay. Had it really looked that much different when the Mejias cleaned the place? Now he wasn't so sure. It had been cloudy and overcast the last few weeks—maybe that was the reason the floor didn't shine. The Mejias had worked there in the autumn, which had been dry and sunny. The place might have looked better simply because the rooms were filled with light. If the place looked dingy, it might be because it *was* dingy: small, built with cheap materials and in need of a fresh coat of paint.

When the Nicaraguans finished, he doubled the normal tip. When he offered to help them carry their things, they declined. The two women trudged down the steps to their car, carrying their buckets, brooms and vacuum cleaner.

I see, said the blind man. How petty he had been. How pusillanimous. This was it; this was what he had feared when he first engaged the cleaning service. He had treated them the way he had always seen people treat domestic servants, particularly non-white female servants: with that same authoritarian condescension.

He went into the bedroom and fell face down on the bed that had just been done by the maids. The smell of the fresh linen and the clean touch of the sheets mocked him; the crisp sound of the cloth when he moved was a snicker that chided him without words.

His trial was set to begin in the three weeks, and he wasn't ready. It wasn't that his lawyer hadn't prepared him well for all the legal possibilities; that wasn't the issue. It was his guilty frame of mind that needed work. He had learned something in the past weeks: how a clever lawyer could use a defendant's guilty feelings against the defendant on the stand, even if that defendant wasn't actually guilty of the charges but, like Kaiser, merely guilty of *something*. If he had to face down Tulsky and McGinnis feeling the way he felt today, his butt was barbecue.

In order to be ready, he had to get square with himself, within himself. He needed a test to pass, though he wasn't sure what kind. He needed a trial before the trial. He needed to know the worst about himself, and he needed to know the best. Something, he wasn't sure what, needed to be confronted. Something, he wasn't sure what, needed to be laid to rest. He needed to try to do a good deed, the kind of deed that, as people are so fond of saying, never goes unpunished.

He turned over in bed and looked at the bookcase at the end of the room. There, at the right side corner of the top shelf, were the books, videos and DVDs by Cuban exile authors that Ricardo had given him. The week before the trial was spring vacation; he wouldn't have to cancel any classes.

It was time to return to Cuba.

XIII

To: PLUME International Writers Society
420 Bradley Place
Los Angeles, California

Dear Sir or Ms.,

I wish to cancel my membership in PLUME. I am distressed by the universal acceptance and constant usage, by organizations such as PLUME, Amnesty International and the United Nations, of the term human rights—meaning exclusively political and free speech rights. Isn't the right to eat a human right? Isn't medical attention a human right? I find it appalling that countries like Cuba and China, which at least acknowledge a responsibility for the survival of the individual citizen, have a worse human rights record than Brazil or India, where people are allowed to die in the street.

Just as countries that deny political and free speech rights should be pressured to open their systems, so nominal democracies, including the USA, should be equally pressured to provide the minimum necessities for survival for all their citizens. Freedom of the press and literary freedom mean little to those who are totally preoccupied with the struggle to survive. Until human rights organizations recognize the relief of lethal poverty as a human right, they cannot truly claim any moral authority.

Yours truly,
Jack Kaiser

P.S. Don't worry about refunding me the balance of this year's dues.

How they would laugh when they read his letter at the PLUME office. They might check the roll and discover that his qualification for PLUME membership rested upon a partial credit on the screenplay of an obscure film two decades earlier. *We got some real crazies in this organization*, the reader would say as the crumpled wad arched toward the trash basket.

Still, he felt better when he slipped the letter into the mailbox. Now he was ready to smuggle prohibited literature into Cuba.

*   *   *

He was going to Havana again, and that meant another trip to Tijuana as well. Because Tijuana, among all its other forbidden delights (*Welcome to Tijuana / Tequila sexo marihuana* the Euro-rocker Manu Chao sings) was also the gateway to Cuba. In Kaiser's mind, the two cities were intimately linked. How appropriate that this town, which had grown from a tiny Mexican pueblo into a big city by servicing thirsty gringos back when the US was dry, should be the entry portal to the latest prohibited paradise.

Flying from LA meant making complicated and uncertain connections through a third country. Everyone he knew who had gone to the The Island, legally or illegally, had gone on the direct flight out of TJ. The windows of all the travel agencies on Revolución blazoned posters of a lovely Cubana walking toward you out of the surf, her wet dress plastered tightly to her body. They never questioned the legality of your status when you bought your ticket; that was between you and the US government and none of their business.

So again he drove the familiar route down the 405 to Mexico, but instead of crossing the border in his car, he parked on the American side, wheeled his suitcase through the steel gates into Mexico and grabbed a taxi. He was early, and he momentarily considered a quick pit stop at the Frontera, but he decided to let it go—maybe on the return trip.

*   *   *

He checked in well ahead of schedule and took a seat at his departure gate. He noticed that the room was slowly, in groups of two and three, beginning to fill up with people dressed entirely in white—Santeros, practitioners of Santería. They were clothed in white linen, they wore white shoes, and they all wore some type of head covering, painter's caps for the men and bonnets or white headwraps for the women. Some of them carried bundles of what looked like twigs and weeds. This had happened once before on one of Kaiser's flights—they were all headed to some kind of confab in Cuba, which apparently was HQ for all those who worshiped the Orishas, the divinities of the faith.

Unfortunately, the TJ-Havana direct flight was a red-eye both ways, and Kaiser couldn't sleep on planes. He browsed the books in his bag. He'd read the travel guides cover-to-cover on earlier trips. That left the contraband materials. He was a little wary of taking them out on the plane: surely there were security people aboard. But the seat next to him was occupied by a seventy-year old woman who was sound asleep; not at all likely to be an agent of the Cuban secret police.

He began discreetly looking through his forbidden cargo. He had become quite a Cubaphile in the last couple of years, so he recognized every book. *Mea Cuba* he had already read in English: a collection of essays by Guillermo Cabrera Infante, probably Cuba's most celebrated literary exile until the recent fame of the late Reinaldo Arenas. And there was indeed one of Arenas's novels in his bag, *El Palacio de Los Blanquisimas Mofetas*. Arenas was probably at the tip-top of the list of unwelcome authors on the island. The writer's homosexuality would no longer pose a problem for the government (at least according to the publicly declared policy) but his criticism of the revolution would be less welcome than ever, now that he had been the subject of a Hollywood movie. Sure enough, that very film, *Before Night Falls*, was one of the videos in his bag. Kaiser imagined an interrogator waving the video in his face, while Kaiser sat in a wooden chair under a low-hanging naked bulb.

There was also a copy of the documentary film *Improper Conduct*, about the Cuban government's suppression of gays in the sixties and seventies, which had been made by the late Nestor Almendros, cinematographer of lush films like Malick's *Days of Heaven*. There was a copy of Edmund Desnoes's *Memorias de la Subdesarollo*, which had become the celebrated film called in America *Memories of Underdevelopment*. The book had been published in Cuba, but Desnoes had since emigrated, and the book was now not banned but "unavailable" which amounted to the same thing: it had been pulled from libraries. And most fun of all, there was Pedro Juan Gutiérrez's *Trilogía Sucia de La Habana* (*Dirty Havana Trilogy*), the ultimate depiction of Havana as a rollicking, turbulent sexual jungle. They had allowed him to publish it—but only in Spain.

Why had he accepted this mission? Not only did he believe, as he had written in the letter to PLUME, that the whole human rights debate was myopic, but also, though it was completely unfashionable now to say so, he wasn't so sure the Cuban governments policies couldn't be defended: this wasn't China or vast Russia, this was a little island just off the shore of the most powerful nation in the history of the world, and said powerful nation was essentially at war with the little island. All countries accept reduced personal liberty in time of war.

Another question was: why Rich Goines had selected him for the mission? Did the student think Kaiser was gay? Or in denial that he was gay? Kaiser knew he was homo-paranoid but such attempts to out him had occurred so many times before.

His sister-in-law's family, for instance, had assumed he was gay for years. Typical New York Jews, they were more self-consciously wised-up than a private eye in a pulp novel. They knew what it meant when a fifty-year-old male had never been married. He actually enjoyed throwing them bait at family dinners, i.e. *Heard that new Elton John album? It's great*, and then watching as they flung sly, smug glances at one another across the table: *They knew.*

Even in Cuba, somebody tried to out him. Whenever he had remarked that he wanted to go to Vedado, Silvio, his driver, had needled him, To be with the gays. Then when Kaiser wanted to go to the Tropicana: To see the gays. Or when he drove Kaiser along the eastern end of Quinta Avenida: Maybe you'd like to get out here—with the gays. Kaiser of course recognized the projective nature of the driver's jokes: Arenas had written in his autobiography that he didn't know a single Cuban man, straight or gay, who hadn't had sex with at least one woman, one man, one animal and one vegetable.

Kaiser also understood that he was overly sensitive in this area. There was the incident from a trip to Israel two decades earlier. He had looked up an old high school friend who had always been both openly gay and openly *goy*: not a Jew. That he of all people should end up living in Tel Aviv was a delightful bit of strangeness. He and Kaiser had had dinner and schmoozed until the late hours, when suddenly something (and Kaiser couldn't even remember what, some innocuous remark) had set off Kaiser's paranoid radar. He became anxious that, as had happened so many times in the past, this gay friend would attempt to out him as a repressed gay. Kaiser's discomfort was obvious, and the friend figured out what was going on.

Kaiser had hastily excused himself. Later, he sent a gift and a letter of apology. The friend sent a princely and magnanimous response that Kaiser had always cherished. But he still felt acutely the shame of that moment.

Of course, he was wiser and hipper than that now, wasn't he? Or was he? He recalled the writer Norman Mailer saying on television once that he was now over sixty years old and still being accused of being a latent homosexual.

Of course, the interviewer said, you're beyond being bothered by stuff like that now, aren't you?

I'm *all but* beyond it, Mailer had said.

*   *   *

He managed to doze just briefly before the plane bumped ground. Fuzzy-eyed, he saw to his dismay that their port of arrival was not the big, new terminal, but the tiny old concrete structure nearby.

You had to walk across the landing strip to get to the terminal. There, one had to line up for an inspection. There were three little booths, each captained by an officer (usually a female) in Cuban army green. They would examine your papers and after a time buzz you through into Cuba. Tourists usually got through quickly. It was *emigre* Cubans returning to see family, as Rich Goines's friend Ricardo had said, who usually got the most attention.

But there was a possibility one of the agents might play a hunch and find the goods in Kaiser's bag. What would happen then? He might possibly be questioned and sent back home though they might detain him for quite a while first. They would try to find out for whom the books were intended. That would be their real object of concern.

Kaiser had the card with name and address hidden in one of the Nike's in his suitcase. He knew enough not to keep the card in his billfold. On his last trip, he had gotten a going-over like the one given to Ricardo at this same terminal as he tried to leave the country. A woman in green had pulled him aside into a little room. She had emptied his billfold and found things in it that he didn't even remember were in there: a pass for the research room at the Huntington Library in Pasadena; the address of a cigar store on Santa Monica Boulevard that had been out of business for three years; a condom that had dried to a crisp. He had brought student papers to grade on the trip, and she perused each one page-by-page to make sure he wasn't smuggling out anti-government manuscripts. She had become suspicious when she saw Spanish names on some of the papers; he tried to explain that he had many Mexican students. Fortunately, the papers had all been graded, with his notes in red ink all over them.

This time, however, things went smoothly. The woman at the inspection booth buzzed him through after only a minute or two. On the other side, he found Silvio waiting, wearing the gold guayabera shirt Kaiser had left him as a gift on his last visit. Silvio helped Kaiser put his bags into the trunk of an aging Lada. The cars were virtually the only reminder of the once enormous Russian presence in Cuba.

Enjoying the shirt? Kaiser asked. The guayabera was the classic Cuban shirt, worn tail out, with its pleats, embroidery and four big pockets on the front. Trouble was, it was difficult to get them in Cuba anymore; the revolution hadn't really encouraged the millenary industry. On his last trip, Kaiser had seen Silvio looking enviously at his, which Kaiser had picked up in Tijuana, so he had given it to him as a tip.

I am enjoying it, Silvio said, Of course, I have to be careful where I wear it.

What do you mean?

You don't know? The guayabera is kind of the informal uniform of the MININT men—the Ministry of the Interior.

The secret police?

Sí. At a concert or a fiesta, look around for the guy on the edge of the crowd, wearing the guayabera. And if he has a camera too, well, then you can really be sure.

Kaiser remembered a time when he'd been sitting on the wall of the Malecón when a nearby kid in a Lakers jersey asked him for the time. Kaiser answered in his fractured Spanish, and the kid had begun laughing. *Usted 'parece Cubano*, the boy had said, and Kaiser had wondered why the kid was so damned relieved. Kaiser had been wearing a guayabera, and the kid had undoubtedly assumed he was MININT.

Look, I have some bad news, Silvio said. I have family coming from New York on Tuesday. It was very sudden—they just told me two days ago. It's the only time they can come this year, and they must stay in your place. So you must move on Wednesday—but I found you a very nice place in Vedado.

With the gays?

What? Silvio had apparently forgotten his little joke. No, a doctor and his family. It's cheaper than here and they are very nice. You'll like it.

Whatever.

Things are a bit looser these days with the girls, Silvio told him. Not so much *policía*.

But once they arrived at the house Kaiser was renting, the driver told a slightly different story. I want to tell you some things, he said. It's not all fun and games with the girls now. Things have changed. I don't want you keeping any girl here overnight. Watch her at all times. Don't let her see where you keep the money. The girls know that Americans carry a lot of cash because their credit cards are no good. When you're done, call her a cab and wait with her until it comes.

My God, thought Kaiser. You're making it sound as though she was some kind of prostitute.

He was distracted from these thoughts by the exploration of his new digs. The place had two bedrooms, a full kitchen, a parlor and a bath, but the real kick was the furniture. Kaiser hadn't seen so many antiques since he'd left Alabama: mirrors in scalloped mahogany frames, tables with legs carved into the shape of lion's paws, an armchair with a spread-winged falcon for a backrest and birds talons for the arms. It made sense that Havana would be flush with antiquities: so many wealthy Cubans had fled the island, leaving so much behind. And all the years since, the island had been off-limits to American buyers.

When he awakened the next morning, he called the telephone number he had been given for Lázaro Perdomo. No one answered. He let it ring and ring just to be sure. Maybe the man had moved (though people in Havana almost never moved) and he wouldn't have to deliver the bloody books after all. That would be a relief.

Silvio and his wife served him breakfast beside the pool. Kaiser's host was a bear-like man with big black-framed glasses. His thick body was ideally served by the loose guayabera shirt. Silvio's fleshy face cried out for a beard, but for some reasons Cubans avoided beards. He couldn't remember having seen a single one on the street.

Over breakfast, he got to know a good deal more about Silvio than he had learned on his last visit. Trained as an aeronautical engineer, he had married a Russian woman while studying in Odessa and returned with her to Cuba. He directed Kaiser's attention to the little one-room shotgun shack beside the swimming pool, with its roof of corrugated metal like the ones Kaiser knew from the rural south in the USA. Silvio had lived there with his wife when he first returned from Russia; now it was used only for storage. With the help of a couple of paid workers, Silvio had then built the two-story duplex houses, one to rent out and one to occupy, as well as a stone patio, barbecue pit and swimming pool. And he was buying up real estate in the Marina Hemingway area.

I didn't think an individual could buy real estate in Cuba.

It's difficult, but it can be done. The system is opening up just a little. People are trying to get positioned for when the day comes. I'm prepared to wait. If it takes him two years to die, I'll wait two years; if it takes ten, I'll wait ten.

A bit later, he got Silvio to drive him into town, to the La Corona cigar factory.

This fucking country, the driver said, is so fucking crazy. Some bastard is trying to claim that the land I live on is his. Yes, the place where you are staying. This was not like the houses I bought. I inherited this property from my father. I have papers and everything. Yet this bastard is taking me to court. I have to see a lawyer today.

Don't talk to me about legal problems, Kaiser said. You'll get no sympathy here.

Then Kaiser attempted to speak about his own legal problems in Spanish.

Please, the driver said. I speak excellent English.

But I wanted to practice my Spanish.

Look, you know a little Cuban history, don't you? Well, what General Weyler did to Cuba, you are doing to the Spanish language.

That bad?

Worse. Weyler only burned down half of Cuba.

He had Silvio leave him at the La Corona factory. He bought a box of Hoyo Double Coronas; then he walked over to Partagas and got a box of 8-9-8s. He walked through Habana Vieja, just getting lost and taking photos. He went to a house that was a museum dedicated to Alejo Carpentier, and the scene of one of his greatest novels. On Calle Obispo, he found a seat on the terrace of an upstairs café, had lunch and smoked one of the Partagas. He looked out at the rooftop panorama of the four-hundred-year old buildings crowned with potted plants, dovecotes, clotheslines hung with fresh wash, and A-frames in which people lived. Two different strains of *son* music played by combos in a couple of the cafes below competed for his attention.

It has happened again, he reflected as he smoked. Here in Cuba, he had again been overwhelmed by the actual, by the simple reality of things. When you're young, you're constantly startled into awareness by the vividness of the real. The whole world's a savior, went an old Doors song. But as you get older, you learn to see the sameness of things and reality loses its power to amaze. Before his first trip to Cuba, he thought that he had forever lost the capacity for surprise, but he had been wrong. Now, once again, he could feel the bracing, restorative strangeness of this place, and he was reminded that there was a world completely outside his trial and his troubles.

But almost immediately something began to gnaw at him. It was the books and Lázaro Perdomo. He wasn't too far from the man's address.

So he went back up Obispo to the Prado, and walked along the mall until he reached Trocadero Street, which was in a terrible state even by Havana standards. There were chuckholes the size of watermelons and big piles of rubble hunks. There was an old green Buick on one side of the street and a blue car with silver trim on the other that Kaiser didn't at first recognize. When he got closer, he realized it was a DeSoto, the first one he'd seen in at least forty years, with the tiny replica of the conquistador's helmet mounted on the front of the hood.

In front of the address he was looking for, two old black men played dominoes at a table beside the doorway. The one facing the building had a gray mustache and wore a blue baseball cap and a T-shirt with the face of Camilo Cienfuegos on it; his adversary wore an old Panama and a black shirt with white stripes. He smoked a cigar as he studied the white tiles. Behind him was another pile of rubble: plaster shards that had been swept out of the hallway.

Kaiser greeted them. The men looked up and smiled as the returned the salutation.

Ustedes conocen Lázaro Perdomo?

It was like winter had suddenly come to the tropics. The two men both instantly dropped their eyes and started shaking their heads.

No, no, no lo conozco, was all they would say.

Inside the building, he walked up a dangerously decrepit stairway to the second floor, where he found the designated apartment, 2B. He rang the bell a few times, then started knocking. No answer. The door of the apartment behind him opened just a crack, and he turned and saw a woman's eyes peeking around the edge.

Buscando Lázaro Perdomo, he said. The door slammed shut, and he could hear the safety latch slide quickly into place.

On the way out of the building, he passed a stout woman coming in with groceries. One more try: *Conoce Lázaro Perdomo?* And again the diverted eyes, and the head shaking no, no, no.

Quite obviously this guy Perdomo was in some kind of deep *mierda*—a political dissident, undoubtedly, and under surveillance by the authorities. The only good news for Kaiser was that the man might have gone underground and vanished. Maybe he wouldn't have to deliver the books after all.

He caught a cab in front of the old capitol building. The cabby was a stocky guy with a big mustache. He spoke good English and asked Kaiser what he'd been doing, and he mentioned he'd visited the museum in the house of Carpentier, Cuba's most important novelist. It turned out that the driver was, of all things, a professor of literature.

I knew some people who knew Carpentier, the driver said. Carpentier was mean; a very unpleasant man.

Kaiser had heard that, too. In fact, he had read it in the English translation of Cabrera Infante's memoir *Mea Cuba*, one of the books he'd just brought into the country.

Nobody liked him, Kaiser said. I read that. You know, when I read *The Lost Steps—Los Pasos Perdidos*—I kept thinking this is a good story, but the hero is such an asshole, a real *pendejo.*

The cabbie laughed.

And I could never figure out, does the author know? Does he know the character is a *pendejo*, or is the author a *pendejo* himself?

I've never read that book. What was the character like? Why was he so bad?

His stupid attitudes toward women, Kaiser said. He basically abandons his girlfriend in a foreign country without a second thought once she ceases to amuse him.

The cabby chuckled. So if the hero is a *pendejo*, it's not a good novel.

Not necessarily. All of Faulkner's protagonists, for instance, are deeply flawed. But the author is not identifying himself with any of them.

I see. Cervantes is not Quixote. He would be, except for one thing: Cervantes knows Quixote is loco, and Quixote does not know.

That's it. Well, with Carpentier, I'm not sure if he knows or not.

Listen, how long are you going to be in town? Give me a ring. We can have dinner and talk.

Kaiser took the man's card. Touching, really, how starved the driver was for intellectual conversation with the outside world.

They drove along the curving Malecón and he saw again the favorite cliché image of Havana presented by American TV news—the beautiful seascape beyond the wall juxtaposed against the devastated old buildings on his left. And Kaiser found himself thinking that, despite all the problems, life in Cuba still seemed materially better for more people than any other Latin American country he'd ever visited. It was stupid that the government didn't let in more outside media—let Cubans see what life was like in Lima, in Mexico City, in Kingston, in Port au Prince, in Spanish Harlem—in that company, Havana didn't look so bad.

Once back at Silvio's, he swam and took a nap. He ate dinner at a nearby *paladar* (private restaurant) in Marina Hemingway. By eleven-thirty, he was ready for some club-hopping.

The new place to go is Cabaret Lumumba, Silvio said. Beautiful women; nice clothes. But you better be ready to spend some money.

They drove past Marina Hemingway. Then everything got very dark. There were no streetlights.

You noticed the change, huh? Silvio said. Infra-red cameras in the trees all around. You-Know-Who's house is nearby. If I stopped the car and got out, we'd have a lot of company really fast.

They went through a gate and pulled up to the club, which was part of a complex of stores and restaurants. Silvio pointed, and Kaiser walked past the Mercedes and vintage Americans parked all around the front door.

Inside, the Tropicana-style show was winding up. There were the usual showgirls with elaborately plumed headdresses and lithe male dancers with lavender tails and top hats. How idiotic that the government had ever tried to clamp down on gays. Havana without gay culture would be like San Francisco without gay culture: inconceivable.

Once the cabaret had ended, people began to mill about, and Kaiser could now see which women were without escorts. They stood in their long party dresses all around the circular bars that ringed the dining area and dance floor.

One woman was particularly gorgeous. A light-skinned brunette in a black dress, she had him groping for movie-star comparisons: a synthesis of Demi Moore and Jennifer Connelly was the best he could do. He watched her bum a cigarette off some tourist guys next to her. She was attempting to chat them up, but they wanted no part of her. Young fools, thought Kaiser (they were about the girl's own age, mid-twenties). All they could see was some club whore. When they got older, they'd learn to use their eyes.

Kaiser actually experienced an attack of shyness at the thought of approaching her. His mouth was tacky and he had to take a leak. He headed for the restroom where he relieved himself and standing before a mirror, ran a comb through his unmussed hair and tugged on his Hawaiian shirt, the one with the floral bursts on a blue background, so that it would show a bit more chest hair at the base of his neck.

When he returned to the ballroom, however, he found that the woman had already been nailed. She was sitting at a table in the shadows at the edge of the patio with a fat, Teutonic-looking tourist. A real Hollywood Nazi, this one: not the wiry, lipless uniformed SS officer with the high, tight collar, but the Quisling collaborationist bureaucrat, Charles Laughton or Albert Dekker. He had straight blond hair and wire-framed spectacles, and he wore an absurd pale striped tropical suit that did indeed look like something out of an old film. Sure enough, in his lap was a white Panama with a red band. Pathetic. This pudgy old predator had come to Havana to chase after women half his age.

It occurred to Kaiser that someone might make the same judgment upon him. He might even be older than Mr. Quisling, and his Hawaiian shirt might appear more ludicrous than his rival's striped suit.

He waited awhile, hoping that the negotiations might prove unfruitful, but it appeared that the lady and the fat man were an item for this evening. He looked around to see if there was something else nice to latch onto, but many of the girls had already left for the evening and none of those who remained caught his eye. Perhaps it was just that he wanted to hold onto his disappointment. He felt an attack of that's-the-story-of-my-life self-pity coming over him, and since he had learned to avoid those at all costs, he left the club and took a cab home.

Back at his apartment, he lay awake for quite some time. He fell asleep, and woke up a couple of hours later and at first didn't know where he was. It hit him after a few seconds. Cuba; I'm in Cuba. What the fuck am I doing in Cuba just a week before the trial?

*   *   *

Kaiser spent the next day shopping for CDs. Much of what he saw in the store bins was actually available in the US, due to the fact that artistic and cultural products, unlike rum and cigars, were exempt from the economic embargo. And the Cuban CD prices weren't much of a bargain either, only a couple of bucks less than the United States. This time he had

Silvio drop him off at a new store: the one in the fabled Egrem Studios on Quinta Avenida. Here was where it all came from: This was where every Cuban musician of the current era laid down his tracks. But he was disappointed to find the CD selection no bigger than elsewhere in Havana. Distribution and stocking of retail inventory were vexed operations under total socialism. Old was mixed with new; ancient reissues of 40's *conga* rubbed up against the *timba* of the 90's; the only order was alphabetical. The silver lining in all this chaos was that there was little overlap. You invariably found different CDs in every store.

In the years since his first visit, Kaiser had immersed himself in Cuban culture. He'd read every book on the shelf about Cuban history, and every work of fiction by a Cuban author in English—both dissidents like Cabrera Infante and supporters of the regime like Carpentier. He'd similarly begun the exploration of Cuban music. But that was quite a different chore than the books. The library shelves were finite. But Cuban music was boundless; bottomless. The deeper you went, the more there was to know. He had put in as many hours of listening as he had spent researching his entire dissertation, and he still felt something less than a novice.

Sure, he could describe the general contours of Afro-Cuban musical history, beginning with the *son* in the 1920's which Americans mistakenly called rumba, then the conga, nightclub music of the 30's, the mambo in the 50's, Pérez Prado, Benny Moré, then cha-cha-cha and Latin jazz and, after the revolution, salsa and now timba. But these were just the main currents: There were so many tributaries.

One day he would make the pilgrimage to Santiago in the east, Cuba's oldest and second largest city. In musical terms, if Havana was the New York/Los Angeles, where the artists performed and recorded. Santiago was the combined Nashville and Memphis, where they actually came from and learned their craft.

Here in the Egrem bins he found albums by Silvio Rodriguez, the king of the *trovadors*, by Celina Gonzales whose *Santa Barbara (Que Viva Changó)* in the 1940's had publically revealed what everyone already knew—that the Catholic saints in Santería were actually stand-ins for the West Indian divine beings called *Orishas*. There was an album by a contemporary group called Sierra Maestra that did updates of the original *son*, and an item that he'd long sought, a CD by his favorite current group, NG La Banda, containing the classic song *La Bruja*. When his bag of CD's got so big it became unwieldy, he knew it was time to go.

He was now impatient, waiting for the night in order to make another club crawl. He couldn't understand what had gotten into him the night before, why it had to be just that one woman. This was Cuba, the sexual cornucopia. You just keep looking until you find something else.

*   *   *

In fact, that night he decided not to go back to Lumumba's. He told Silvio to drop him at Jimmy's, his playpen from the last trip. This meant a long drive in from Marina Hemingway along Fifth Avenue, with the occasional woman standing on the grassy median, looking for an evening's entertainment. Silvio stopped for a girl and when he dropped Kaiser at Jimmy's, he drove off with her for a quickie in the car.

Inside the bar, the pace was slow. The place was full of women sitting against the wall, but it was early and few men were around. You couldn't see faces too well because the women were in the shadows, but a tall brunette with a friendly smile came over to Kaiser's table. He told her maybe later. Why? She was pretty. But he was still thinking about the girl from last night. The same when a second girl approached him.

He bolted Jimmy's for the El Capitan, a slightly higher-class disco a bit further up the road back to Marina Hemingway. But when he got there, it was the same story. The music hadn't started yet, but the girls were there and they came up to him sitting at the bar, one two three four five came one after another to cruise him, the last two working as a pair, but it was no good. He couldn't stop thinking about *aquella chica*, the one from the night before.

So he was in a cab again, headed back out to where the houses ended, back to the Cabaret Lumumba. As they stopped to turn off onto the road to the entrance, a motorcycle pulled along side, a kid with his girlfriend on the back. The kid spoke fast Havana Spanish. The driver turned to Kaiser.

He wants to know if we'll give her a ride up to the club. It's just to get her past the gate.

Kaiser said sure. The woman smiled and jumped into the back seat with Kaiser; a big blonde, not unattractive, but a bit heavy at her lower end, which was tight-packed into her blue jeans. She wanted to get through the club gate without a male escort, which was forbidden except for the women approved to work the club, so she needed Kaiser as a ringer. Or maybe not as a ringer, because after the guard at the gate waved them through, she looked at Kaiser, smiled again and then slid over next to him. She began to rub up against the outside of his thigh, still grinning.

She wasn't unattractive. On another night, he might have told the cabby to turn around and take them back to his apartment. But it had to be the woman from last night; only she would do. Cuba was the land of sexual abundance, but he, stupidly, had allowed himself to become fixated on one woman. Then he recalled that many Cuban songs were indeed about romantic obsession : it was the necessary complement, the other side of the erotic plenitude that was such a part of life here.

So he paid the admission for the blonde at the door, but he tried to lose her when they got inside. He was earlier than he'd been the night before; the place was just beginning to fill. There was a live band, an all-woman salsa group; the first he'd ever seen. He looked around over and over, but didn't see his target anywhere. It might just not be one of her nights. No reason to think she'd be there every night. But after all this running about, he vowed he wasn't going to go home alone. He began to look for the big blonde—she owed him a favor. He saw, however, that she'd been pulled over into a corner by an older woman who appeared to be some kind of manager, and who was giving the blonde a nice tongue-lashing. The girl had been spotted as a gate-crasher because she didn't wear the requisite long dress.

*   *   *

Just then the brunette walked past him. This time he didn't dawdle; as soon as she took a place by the bar, he was on her with a loud *Holá*! And in a minute she had taken him over to that same table on the patio where she had sat the night before with the striped-suit fat man, and they were attempting a conversation of sorts. She spoke not a word of English.

Parlez-vous francais? Kaiser tried.

A shake of the head. Not only that, but hers was that incomprehensible rapid-fire Havana Spanish spoken open-mouthed, with tongue out and stationary, as though pinned down with a doctor's wooden depressor, so that lips never move and consonants drop. Kaiser knew he was a disaster when he himself tried to speak Spanish, but sometimes he could understand the language if the speaker spoke slowly enough. That was out of the question here. But Kaiser learned that her name was Saray, a strange name, and he picked up the *cien dollares* clearly enough. When he nodded, she took him by the arm and walked over across the room to the same older lady who had tossed out his blonde friend earlier, and gave her a signal that they were leaving.

In the back seat of the cab outside, Kaiser put his arm around the woman. His chest was heaving with excitement, and he was plenty tipsy. He'd had the obligatory *mojito* at Jimmy's, a *Cuba libre* at the El Capitan and another at Lumumba and again he was overwhelmed by the sheer actuality of it all. They drove past a sign that showed Camilo Cienfuegos leading a bunch of *barbudos* out of the forest underneath the slogan VENCEREMOS! and he looked at the gorgeous thing next to him and realized that she wasn't just Cuban; hell, man, she was Cuba: the *barbudos*, the music, the Santeria magic, the nobility of an island whose spirit was unbroken by four decades of pressure and he began to babble into her uncomprehending Spanish-only ear.

I love this country, know that? You know why the US hates you? It has nothing to do with human rights or any of that shit. He turned and spoke to the cab driver as well. Liberals and conservatives, makes no difference they hate you because you told the USA to go to hell and you got away with it! No Latin American country ever did that! Not ever!

The cabbie spoke only slightly more English than the girl, but he nodded as if he understood. They passed a sign that showed the Cuban flag and the legend *PATRIA O MUERTE / SOCIALISMO O MUERTE*.

The left in America died when it abandoned socialism. You know what we got for a left in the USA? The ACLU. I fuckin' hate the ACLU. Phony limousine liberals!

They passed a sign with a portrait of Jose Marti under a slogan reading *CREEMOS EN NUESTRA REVOLUCION SOCIAL*.

That's what we've got in the US instead of real politics! The ACLU, tree-humping Earth Firsters, anti-smoking and animal rights! Everything is rights, rights, rights, as long as those rights don't effect money and property! Rights, but no justice! The right to complain about your illness, but not a penny for the medicine to treat it! Here, at least people get looked after—

Undoubtedly in an effort to shut him up, the woman turned toward him, placed her hand on his thigh and filled his mouth with her tongue. It was thick and sweet, and she moved it around forcefully. When she withdrew it, he was silent for a moment. Then they passed a sign with the famous frowning image of Che and the slogan CONSTRUIMOS EL HOMBRE NUEVO, and that set him off again.

He saw it all so clearly now. The sexual plenitude of Cuba and its revolutionary ethos weren't a contradiction or paradox after all; no, they were one and the same!

He babbled: The hypocrisy of sexual repression in American political correctness; it's just the old-fashioned Puritanism passed off as left politics. *El Hombre Nuevo* has to be beyond the constraints of their petit-bourgeois . . . their petit-bourgeois . . . their . . .

Mercifully, they were at the gate of Silvio's house and the big sheet-metal walls he had placed around his property. After paying the cabby, Kaiser fumbled unsuccessfully with the key in the lock for what seemed an hour, until finally Saray motioned him aside and smoothly clicked the lock open.

When they got inside, he started to show her around what he thought was a very sharp pad by Havana standards. But if she was impressed, Saray sure didn't show it; she behaved as though she had seen better, and she probably had. When they got to the bathroom, though, she pulled up her dress, squatted on the toilet and took a long piss right in front of him. Now he was really in love.

It didn't last. The very next thing she did was to march into the bedroom, and one by one pull out the drawers in the chest to inspect the contents, like a cop on a bust. Kaiser felt as though he were back in that little room with the customs officer. What kind of contraband did she want?

Then she began to speak, asking for something. He persuaded her to write it down so that he could understand. She wanted *un regalo*, a gift—*un chor*, she said. He couldn't find the word in his Spanish-English Dictionary. She went into the bathroom, and emerged holding the bathing suit he'd left to dry on the edge of the tub. A pair of shorts; that's all she wanted, a bloody pair of gym shorts. She was so disappointed when he told her that those were not shorts, but swim trunks.

Now he knew what she had been searching for. Not contraband, but consumer goods. She wanted America: Hilfiger, DKNY, Ralph Lauren. Just as he had put forth his agenda in the taxi, she was very unapologetically informing him of hers. When she saw his little camera on the bureau, she asked for that as a gift as well. He tried to explain that he needed it until the end of the trip. How tactless she was; didn't she realize that you had to coax things out of people?

Yet her clumsiness spoke for her, and Kaiser understood:

I deserve better than this! I'm young, I'm beautiful, I'm smart, and I deserve better than this! she was telling him. In most any other country in the world, she'd have her pick of men, young good-looking men with future prospects, and her own future might be brighter than theirs. She deserved better than some middle-aged American fugitive, brokedown and just plain broke. Well, she'd get no argument from him.

She spied his cigars. She took one from each box and put them into her bag. Those he let her have.

After such a start, he was expecting the sex to be perfunctory at best. She surprised him with her controlled enthusiasm. He kissed her up and down the length of her body, which was quite as beautiful as he had expected, until he found himself between her legs, ready to snack. But he raised his head; she pressed it down again. She wanted it; he had thought he did, too. But he found himself hesitant. He realized it was a kind of shyness; he wasn't yet ready for such intimacy with a woman who'd been searching his belongings ten minutes earlier. Impatiently, she took his hand and shoved a finger into her pussy. She showed him where the sweet spot was. He remembered the first woman who had shown him that spot, decades earlier. He had been preoccupied with his own performance in recent months, and he needed reeducation in the topography of the cunt. Understandably, none of the women he'd been with in the last year had considered such lessons a part of their job description. Each time he touched the spot, he could feel that heartbreaking little quiver run through her whole body.

Then they did some fucking. She sighed and moaned, but Kaiser thought she was probably faking. He didn't feel that quiver of response he'd just learned to recognize. It was nice of her to feign it, though.

Though they tried several different positions, he experienced his usual difficulty finishing. He even put on a fresh condom so she could give him a blow job and that didn't work. He pulled off the rubber and was about to ask her to finish him off *a mano* when she began speaking to him. It took him a while to puzzle out her meaning, but eventually he realized she was telling him to call a cab, and to go take a shower while she waited.

We take a shower? Kaiser asked. *Ambos*?

No. Tu solamente.

Shit. He remembered what Silvio had warned him about. She wanted to get him in that shower so she could lift something. And he was just beginning to really like her, too.

You want to steal something, eh? You know all Americans carry cash, don't you?

Again she smiled at him in incomprehension. He felt no anger, nor did he feel he was patronizing her by not getting mad. It was just the way things were in her world. But he didn't let her out of his sight after that, not for a second, as they dressed and he called the taxi. Then she surprised him yet again. He was telling her that he was a teacher of literature and he showed her the book he was reading, Jose Saramago's *Baltasar and Blimunda*. She asked him to give her a call sometime, and wrote her phone number on the first page of the paperback, even drawing a little map so that he could find her apartment in Marianao. He hadn't expected this; he'd been pretty much of a dud sexually and more importantly, he surely didn't show any sign of being a cash cow or sugar daddy.

*　　*　　*

As they waited on the front porch, he thought she looked so sad. She held something in her hand: her government ID card. Apparently she had to show it to the cabby. When she left, he went back and checked the phone number she had written in the book. Why not call her again? She was still the most beautiful woman he'd ever been with, thief or not. Her dark eyes revealed genuine profundity of feeling.

XIV

The next day was his day to move out of Silvio's and into the Vedado apartment. Silvio also had what he thought would be good news.

I've found you a driver. Twenty-five dollars a day plus gas. She will be available twenty-four hours a day, no matter where you want to go.

Did you say she?

Yes. A Russian woman.

I don't know, Silvio. I mean, it's a little awkward—a woman driving me around all night while I look for *chicas*.

Pah! Don't worry about it. This is Cuba! You have to get used to the way we do things here.

But Kaiser didn't feel comfortable with it, and he felt even less so when the driver arrived to pick him up an hour later. She was a large woman from Ukraine with bobbed reddish hair and a round face. Her name was Olga. She spoke little English, but was fluent in Spanish. She had married a Cuban student and emigrated here during *la guerra fría*. The marriage was over, but Olga had remained.

As they drove away from Silvio's, Kaiser began to sing one of the few Cuban songs whose lyrics he knew by heart:

Pica—no pica

She joined in with him: *Los tamalitos que vende Olga, Olga.*

What did she do other than drive tourists around?

Soy una profesora, she said. *Una profesora de fisica y matematicas.*

Ouch. She was a teacher like him, but here professors had to drive horny tourists around to make a few extra bucks. Later, as they drove through the tunnel that connected Havana to the eastern suburbs, she further elaborated that she wasn't able to find work as a teacher, so she had begun working as a secretary for the last few years.

In Guanabacoa, he first went to the Santería Museum, which was a bit of a disappointment. The really deep stuff was top secret, for initiates only, and most of what was on display covered elements of the African faith that Kaiser already knew. There was one exception: he hadn't realized that the little figures of the Orisha divinities that people carried with them for luck or placed upon homemade altars to be placated with gifts were sometimes called, of all things, Lázaros.

The African Market turned out to be closed on Tuesdays; that still left the old Jewish cemetery. The graveyard was impressive; as in the famous and much larger one in Havana, many of the graves were marked by sculptures and monuments of white marble. He was startled to see how many of the dead had perished in their thirties and forties. Life had been short in the tropics, even well into the twentieth century. The dates of death cut off around the time of the revolution. Most of Havana's once-large Jewish community had emigrated.

He was thinking, as he wandered with camera among the tombs, about Saray, the way she had brazenly rummaged through his things the night before. She deserved better than him, as he had realized the night before. He was still sure that she had meant to steal, but that didn't bother him, either. Her tactlessness now seemed to him quite touching, a sign of innocence. Should he pursue a further relationship? He knew stories of American men who maintained Cuban girlfriends that they visited a few times a year. Some had even managed to get the girls off the island and into the US.

The cemetery faced out upon one of those lovely green valleys that characterize the Cuban landscape. Maybe, he thought, instead of trying to get her into the US, he should stay here. It all seemed so far away now: his job, his court case, his past. He could ask for political asylum, as a number of American fugitives had done. Veronica, Tulsky, McGinnis, the Student League for the Suppression of Horny Old Men: Fuck them all.

Oh yes, that was all he needed: to be alone and broke in a country where he didn't speak the language and had no knowledge of how to juice the system to get what he wanted. No matter in what country you lived, you had to know how to juice the system to get what you wanted.

Olga drove him back into the city, to his new apartment. He sighed when she turned off the Malecón and stopped at a blue apartment building he knew well: it was the same one where he had stayed on his last trip when he had had his run-in with the *policía*.

At least the apartment was different. When he knocked, a girl who appeared to be in her middle teens answered. Another Cuban stunner. Dark-chocolate eyes and long brown hair cascading over her shoulders. She fetched her mother, a thin, friendly woman with glasses and short gray hair. The lady introduced him to her other house guest, a sunburnt Italian in soccer club T-shirt and shorts. Then she showed Kaiser to his bedroom and bathroom.

The place was clean and trim, like all the apartments he'd stayed in in Havana. There was a patio that looked out on Calzada. This was the television room. Back in the living room, there was the usual antique furniture, some large potted tropical plants and, something he hadn't seen in the apartments he'd stayed in before, shelves and shelves of books. Many were medical texts, but others were literature and politics.

Kaiser here encountered the first true believers he'd met in Cuba. The psychiatrist with whom Kaiser had stayed before had never mentioned politics, and he had had a Christmas tree in his living room, still a bit daring by Cuban standards. Silvio was a child of the revolution who had become cynical, the result of his service in the Cuban army's Angolan adventure. *Here is Cuba, a country that needs so many things . . . what were we doing in Africa?* he had said to Kaiser. Most people seemed to have mixed feelings about the system and its leader. They by no means saw themselves as the serfs of totalitarianism portrayed in US propaganda, but they wanted to see some changes. Here in the home of Dr. Barranco, however, revolutionary fervor continued to burn undiminished. A framed poster celebrated the victorious *barbudos* entering the capital, guns raised in triumph. On another wall was a framed photograph of Che—not a famous picture, but one Kaiser had never seen before. The revolutionary himself was holding a camera and was about to take a picture, simultaneously creating history and recording it.

Some of the books on the shelves were in English. Kaiser asked if he could borrow one, an anthology of Che's writings, which he placed on the desk in his room.

That night, after Sra. Barranco served him dinner, he met the doctor himself: a tall, thin, gray-headed man who nervously chain-smoked. Kaiser couldn't remember the last time he'd seen a doctor with a cigarette.

And the daughter—her name was Cecilia. She was doing her schoolwork in a rocker out on the patio while her mother watched tonight's *telenovela* serial episode. It was the only dramatic show of the evening on state TV, stuck in the midst of propaganda, local news and cultural fare, so Cubans watched it compulsively. Kaiser tried to take in a little of it, but his attention was drawn to Cecilia bent over a math problem, her long dark hair swept to one side so that it covered her right arm. What a doll. He would have to come back in a couple of years. In a couple of years . . .

A visitor joined them: Cecilia's boyfriend from school. Despite the embargo that kept American fashions from reaching Cuba directly, Cuban kids dressed in much the same hip-hop styles as American kids. He wore a T-shirt, sneakers and a baseball cap turned around backwards; a red cap with the letter M on it for the Matanzas team in the Cuban baseball league.

By now it was time for Kaiser to make the night rounds. He intended to call the number given him by Saray to set up a rendezvous before she left for the Lumumba club. But when the time came, he found himself restless, not sure that he was ready to see her again. Instead, he called Olga and had her take him to the El Capitan, one of the other discos he'd visited the night before. He could have actually had Olga sit in the car and wait for him outside of the club; that was part of the deal when you engaged a driver in Havana. But instead he told her that her services would not be required until the next morning. He couldn't abide the thought of her in the front seat (Big Mama, always watching) while he groped a *chica* in the back.

Inside the club, he took a seat at the bar and the women came by again, presenting themselves and chatting him up. He said *Quizás un poco mas tarde* to three or four girls and then bit on a pretty blonde in blue jeans with a big bust and a tiny waist. She spoke excellent English, too. Outside, there were taxis waiting.

What's your name? Kaiser asked her as they sped back to Vedado.

Mei-ling.

Mei-ling? Mei-ling? She was the least Asian in appearance of anyone Kaiser had ever seen in his life.

All right, then. Mei-ling it is.

They passed the billboard that read *CONSTRUIMOS EL HOMBRE NUEVO*.

I believe in the Cuban Revolution, he said. I really do.

She looked at him as if he was *un poco loco*. Fortunately, tonight he'd had only one drink.

I'm sorry, he said. When I feel sexy, I start talking about la política.

Or was it talking about *la política* that made him feel sexy?

As they pulled up to the apartment building, he noticed that she, like him, was looking all around for police.

I know this building, she said. I've been here before. He paid the cabby, and they ran inside quickly, just in case someone on patrol came around the corner. The Barranco apartment was quiet and dark; the family had retired for the night. When they got to his bedroom and stripped, he grabbed a handful of her long blonde hair and pulled her face gently towards his own. She froze.

I don't kiss, OK? If you want to kiss me, you can kiss me on the neck and below.

Won't kiss? A girl who wouldn't kiss was something he had never encountered in Cuba. So was his next surprise: she had shaved her pussy clean. Unlike some men, Kaiser didn't find this erotic in the least. He wanted to reach for talcum powder and a diaper. All during the taxi ride, he had fantasized about going down on her; but now, no way.

Refusal to kiss and a shaved crotch were marks of professionalism, not romance. Silvio had been right. Things had changed. Cuba was beginning to seem like Tijuana. Like prostitution.

The worst was yet to come. He crawled on top of her and felt her tits; then he sat up in the bed. They had that quality of being a little too firm, a little too pointy. He wasn't sure they were real. Surely this couldn't be true in Havana, the last stronghold of sexual authenticity?

But even so, she was very beautiful. She preferred doggie and he didn't mind because her spine and butt were so shapely. After a while at it, though, he moved away.

You no finish? she asked.

No jugo, he replied.

Goddamit, what was the matter? This wasn't prostitution, this was revolution. Liberating himself from the puritanism of American political correctness was a positive, progressive act. He'd seen it all so clearly the night before. *CONSTRUIMOS EL HOMBRE NUEVO*. He grabbed the book of Che's writings that he'd been looking through earlier in the day, found a page that he wanted, and placed it in front of the girl.

Please read, he said, indicating the lines with his finger. Then he went around behind her and they resumed doing the dog. The woman began reading aloud:

And we will then conclude that almost everything we thought and felt in the past epoch should be filed away, and that a new type of human being should be created. And if each one of us is his own architect of that new human type, then creating that new type of human being who would be representative of the new Cuba will be much easier . . .

She turned her head. You still no finish? Why you no finish?

No jugo, was again all he could say.

She asked to shower afterward. Then she told him how her departure from the building needed to be carefully planned. She would call a taxi; they would wait together inside the building, in the stairwell, until they saw through the glass door that the taxi had pulled up out front. Then she would run out and jump quickly in the cab and make a speedy getaway.

It was all so strange: the government owned the disco; the government allowed the girls to work the place and leave with men. The government owned the taxi that you rode home in. Then the same government would bust you and the girl when you brought her to your place.

Everything in this country was all mixed up.

While waiting there by the stairs, he mentioned a CD by Carlos Varela that he'd bought the other day. Soon, they were having a real conversation about Cuban music; whether NG La Banda was still any good, and how was Arte Mixto now that the singer had defected to the US? She was surprised that he knew Orishas, the top rap group in Cuba.

Why don't you come back to the club? she asked him.

Oh, I don't know; it's kind of late.

Will you be coming again while you're here?

Quizás, quizás, quizás, he quoted a classic Cuban pop song. Then the taxi came up outside, and she made a dash for it.

Her invitation was tempting. She was pretty and energetic and she could probably teach him quite a bit about Cuba. And on a second date, she might even do a little kissing.

*   *   *

The next day at breakfast was heartbreaking in that way that only Cuba can be. After he had finished his ham and eggs, the señora asked him, very abashed, if he could pay for the two nights he'd spent at the house so far. This was a breach of Cuban etiquette: normally, the bill was never presented until the end of the stay.

First, Kaiser wondered if he had done something wrong, but the señora explained to him the reason: the doctor was going to Camaguey for several days to work in a clinic there, and he wanted to have some folding money for the journey.

That was painful. This was a middle-class physician, a guy who would have a fat Beverly Hills practice back home. But in Cuba, he was living so close to the bone that he had to beg a cash advance from his guest in order to have pocket change for a trip. The doctor himself was out on the porch, looking down at the street, smoking. Although he could hear the conversation from the dining room behind him, he never turned around.

*   *   *

Despite the sinister and frustrating experience he'd had the first time, Kaiser decided to make another effort to find the elusive Lázaro Perdomo. He called the number again and a woman's voice answered. She didn't speak English, and her Spanish was as impenetrable to him as his was to her. All he could deduce was that Perdomo wasn't there. His ability to read and write Spanish, however, was better than his ability to speak it. If he went again to the apartment, he could communicate with the woman with pen and paper.

He had Olga drop him off at the La Corona factory, not at the Perdomo address, because he didn't want her to know what he was up to. Everybody here worked for the government in one way or another, so you couldn't be too careful. He had an espresso in the lounge of the factory store, and set out on foot.

Outside the factory, he stopped a moment to watch the activity across the street, behind the Museum of the Revolution. A teacher was putting a class of kids through a marching drill. The kids all wore their school uniform. In Cuba, very young children wear a white shirt with a cranberry-red bandanna and, depending on sex, either shorts or a skirt in the same cranberry shade. These kids, however, were a bit older, perhaps twelve or thirteen, and their shirts were yellow with a bandanna that matched the brown color of their shorts or skirts. Their coach was a big black man in a bright yellow T-shirt and Bermuda shorts. He had the kids lined up double-file. For a while they'd march toward Kaiser; then the coach would bark something and they'd spin around in unison and march back the other way. When he blew his whistle, they stopped still at attention.

When at the same age as these kids, he had hated regimentation and authority. It would have been hell, sheer hell, for him to grow up in such a society, where education had become militarized.

But this, as was the case with so many things on this island of locos, led straight back to the Cuban Conundrum. In Cuba, you had a government that was intrusively, overbearingly present in people's lives; in almost every other Latin American country, you had governments that paid no attention to their citizens at all. In Colombia or Peru or Guatemala, there would be no marching, no uniforms, but also very probably, no school and no clean clothes of any kind. In Rio and Medellin, the males in this group might already be living on the street, surviving by petty theft and drug sales.

He began to think again that most blasphemous thought, the one unacceptable to both the right and the left in his home country: that history might look back one day in the distant future and say that the wrong side won the Cold War. He wasn't drunk, either; not like the other night in the taxi with Saray. He had come to this conclusion not because Cuban communism was so good, but because the alternative for so many of the world's poorest countries seemed even worse.

He wandered back to the address on Trocadero Street. The Buick and the DeSoto were not only parked on the same block, and as near as he could tell, they hadn't moved an inch. Likewise, the two old guys playing dominos outside the house; they had on exactly the same clothes and the cigar in the mouth of the man with the old Panama was exactly the same length as before. The heap of plaster shards behind him remained similarly undisturbed.

However, when he knocked on the door of apartment four, this time someone answered. A female voice asked, *Quién es?* and it was not the same voice with which he had spoken on the phone.

Lázaro Perdomo?

He no live here anymore, said the voice on the other side. This woman sounded younger than the first and spoke a bit of English.

You know how I can reach him?

You leave your phone number.

She didn't ask him in or inquire who he was and why he was there, but he was actually relieved that she didn't. The less time spent around this place, the better. He gave her the number of the Barranco family and left.

A bit later he met Olga in front of Partagas and had her take him back to his house. His plan was to grab a towel and bathing suit and head for the nearest beach for the remainder of the day. As he walked through the living room, he noticed the red baseball cap of Cecilia's boyfriend on the dinner table, with its big blue letter M for Matanzas. He heard strange noises as he opened his closet. Well, not that strange; they were the sounds of lovemaking. The other side of the wall was Cecilia's cubby, a tiny servant's bedroom attached to the kitchen. She and the boyfriend had ditched lunch at school to run home for a quickie. Apparently she was good: the boy was the one doing all the yelling. Kaiser grabbed up his things and left as quietly as he could.

On the way out to the beach club, Kaiser asked his Russian driver if she'd seen Andrei Tarkovsky's film *Stalker*.

I saw *Andrei Roublev*, she said.

Yeah, that was his greatest. This was a kind of science fiction film.

What was it about?

Well, in the future there's this Forbidden Zone. At the heart of the zone is this little room. If you go into the little room, you come face to face with your deepest desire. Something so deep within you that you yourself don't know what it is. The only way to find this little room is to get this psychic to guide you. He's what they call the Stalker. These two guys hire him and he guides them to the room. That's the story of the film.

What's in the room?

It's different for everyone. The last guy that the Stalker brought in, what he saw inside the room was so disturbing that he went home and killed himself. It really wasn't that great a movie. I guess I was just thinking about it because you're Russian.

What is your birth sign?

You're kidding. A professor of math and physics doesn't pay attention to that stuff, do you?

She shrugged. Once more Kaiser had observed that in Cuba strange things happen.

The Club Revolución, where Kaiser had had her drive him, had once been the Astoria Club, a yacht club for America's elite. It was still a club for a foreign elite; they just didn't get many Americans these days. For ten dollars, any tourist could buy a daily membership and use the facilities, which included the usual resort amenities: sauna, jacuzzi, swimming pool and a nice little strip of beach, the nicest you were likely to find without driving well outside the city. Kaiser took a dip in the sea, then toweled off and fell apart into a deck chair by the pool.

Next to him was a middle-aged tourist with a NY Yankees cap, smoking a Cohiba. Through designer sunglasses, the man read the latest issue of *Fortune*: WHERE THE MONEY FLOWS blazoned the cover, over a cartoon of a river of greenbacks. A black waiter brought the man a highball in a tall glass; the tourist took the drink without moving his eyes from the magazine. Eventually, the tourist put the magazine away and put down the back of his chair so that he could get some sun. As he stretched out,

Kaiser could for the first time see the design on the man's T-shirt: the angry, staring face of Che was stretched tight across a round belly.

There were beautiful women here, as everywhere in Cuba, but these ladies were foreign tourists, here with men. Kaiser dawdled here for a couple of lazy hours, then cabbed it back to Vedado. When he got to the apartment, he found the door to his bathroom locked.

Just a minute, a female voice inside called. A second later, the door opened and little Cecilia stood before him in a terrycloth robe, her wet hair turbaned up by a red towel.

I'm so sorry, she said. This is supposed to be your bathroom alone, but we're having trouble with the hot water in mine. It's going to be fixed in a couple of hours. I won't bother you again.

He could see the little droplets of water on her legs and feet.

It's OK, he said.

Her robe brushed him as she walked past.

*   *   *

When night came, he had two very attractive options: he could return to the Cabaret Lumumba and Saray, or go to the El Capitan and look up the inexplicably named Mei-Ling. Saray was very beautiful, and he felt certain her quiet facade concealed an interesting mind. Mei-Ling knew everything about Cuban music, spoke English and seemed to be lively and full of fun. Either choice promised a fascinating evening, where he would learn more about the woman and about the country as well.

Instead, though, he went to neither club. He told Olga to drop him off at the Café de Canciones, a basement joint with live bands. He wasn't ready yet for a second encounter with either woman, he thought. He needed a night off to decide which one to go after.

He didn't respond to the advances of any of the women in the Café, either. Those in this club were the most aggressive he had yet encountered; they came up to Kaiser or any other male at the bar and grabbed his ass, pulled his chest hair and pinched his earlobe. Once, walking away from a girl who wouldn't leave him alone, Kaiser passed another who shoved her hand between his legs with such force that he yelped in pain. Enough! He found a table in a dark corner where he could sit unnoticed and just listen to the salsa, which was great, as always.

Tonight was a night to sit and reflect. Time to catch his breath. But he couldn't really think. Something was bothering him, and he wasn't sure what it was. Thinking about Saray or Mei-Ling didn't help, either. He stayed until the first set ended, then took a cab home.

The next day brought more revelations for breakfast. The morning before, he had been served fried eggs. As was his cholesterol-conscious practice, he ate only the whites, leaving the yolks behind. Today, on his plate, he found the whites only. The Barrancos had saved the yolks for themselves. That was another heartbreaker. The place was so beautiful that you forgot sometimes how close to the edge people lived. In Cuba, nothing edible was allowed to go to waste.

What happened next was a shock, too. Cecilia walked past with her books in a backpack. Ciao, she bid him as she went out the door.

Kaiser was jolted: she was wearing the same uniform as the marching kids from yesterday: the yellow blouse, the long tan bandanna, the very short tan skirt. He'd thought she was older, in her late teens. She was certainly mature physically, but her actual age was younger than he'd reckoned.

*   *   *

Olga needed the day off to have her car serviced; Kaiser wandered the streets of Vedado, aimlessly snapping pictures. He walked to the Cohiba Hotel and had a cigar in the lounge. Then he strolled along the Malecón, dodging the occasional huge wave that sloshed over the sea wall. He was restless and distracted, and he still didn't know why. He paused to rest, sitting on the wall, and a big blonde came by. She had enormous tits, barely restrained by a leopard-spotted halter, and she smiled fetchingly. Sexual opportunities were as easy to come by in Cuba as telemarketer phone calls in LA. But he let her pass.

He had some papers to grade. He'd been saving the work for the long wait at the airport on the night of his departure, but he decided to do them now. He went back up to the apartment, which was empty and quiet. The doctor was out of town; the señora was at work, and the Italian house guest was at the beach, where he spent all day every day. Kaiser grabbed up his books and papers. He realized that he still had Dr. Barranco's copy of the selected writings of Che. He took the book and replaced it on the parlor shelf. A few volumes down was a framed picture of Cecilia in a ruffled pink gown, with a bouquet of pink flowers in her hand and a garland of the same around her head. Kaiser recognized the occasion as the celebration of *fiesta de quince años*, the fifteenth birthday at which a girl is allowed to date and entertain marriage proposals.

He set his papers on the glass table on the patio and went about grading, trying to lose his agitation in the discipline of the work. After a couple of hours, he heard the key in the lock and Cecilia came in from school. He waved a hello.

You look a little flushed, he said.

Flushed?

Cecilia spoke excellent English, but the word was unfamiliar to her.

Your face is red. You're breathing hard.

The elevator is broken again. I had to walk up.

She came out to the porch and sat down on the couch beside him. So you teach English?

He nodded. We read some Latin American authors in translation. *Like Water for Chocolate.* And Gabriel García Márquez, *Love in the Time of Cholera.*

He comes here, García Márquez. I saw him one day on the Malecón.

What do you want to study?

Medicine. I want to be a doctor.

Like Che.

Like Dad. Dad knew Che, you know. He always said that Che should have gone back to medicine after the victory of the Revolution. He could have taken charge of the national health system.

Your parents haven't stopped believing. I admire that. I really do.

She seemed to want to change the subject.

What are you working on?

He showed her the paper he was grading, an essay comparing the use of setting to express the authors theme in Faulkner's *A Rose for Emily* and Hemingway's *Soldier's Home.* She had read the Hemingway (no surprise in Cuba, where the writer is venerated) but Faulkner was new to her.

Here: this is very good. Here's where this student points out how Emily's decaying house reflects her sexual obsession. He showed her a page of the paper.

As she leaned over to read, Cecilia's tan bandanna fell across the paper. Kaiser grabbed it by the ends and pulled her face towards him. He put his tongue gently into her mouth. Then he ran his hand up under her skirt.

I accept the sins that are heaped upon me.

And he knew now where he'd been heading all along, why he hadn't gone back to find Saray or Mei-Ling; he saw where he'd been heading not just on this trip, but ever since he'd first visited Cuba two years earlier, and it was almost more than he could bear because he knew now that he was not really looking for intimacy or understanding or relationship or even romance. Not at all. No, it was a different kind of fantasy that he'd been pursuing.

She got up and walked toward Kaiser's bedroom. He followed. He gently laid her across his bed, facing him, and unbuttoned the white cotton blouse of her school uniform. The tan bandanna fell between her breasts. He threw the tan skirt up over her chest and pulled her white panties down to her ankles.

Thank God. There was hair.

Yo creo en la revolución cubana, he said, almost sobbing. *Yo creo en la revolución cubana. Yo creo en la revolución cubana.* Then he lowered his head to her body and stopped speaking.

XV

If you've got to do the time, might as well do the crime.

That's how Kaiser tried to rationalize his behavior; he connected it to the fate awaiting him in his trial in Los Angeles. If you have to do the time, at least do the crime. Or as James Coburn had said in that movie: *I don't want to die innocent.*

But the next morning, he looked down with shame at the eggs upon his plate; the eggs from which the yolks had carefully been excised, and knew himself for what he was: a thief. It was as if he had stolen out of the refrigerator some of the precious food the Barranco family hoarded, or as if he had pilfered from the secret drawer where they kept the hard currency they desperately needed to buy the consumer items that were so difficult to obtain. An American has so much already. Why does he have to take *everything?*

He didn't know if Cecilia had said anything to anyone. The doctor was in Camaguey. The evening before, he had walked past the three of them, when he went out: the mother, Cecilia and the boyfriend, all in front of the TV, watching the nightly serial. The *señora* had given him the usual smile and goodbye wave. Cecilia and the boyfriend had continued watching the TV, not looking at him, but the atmosphere hadn't seemed particularly charged or anxious.

* * *

He went to the jazz club across the street from the Cohiba. The group playing there was dynamite, but he found himself unable to enjoy the music. He went out for a walk along the Malecón. The nearly-full moon sat on the horizon like an egg about to roll off the edge of a table. As he stood leaning against the sea wall, someone walked past behind him and pinched his ass. This time, he didn't even turn around to see who it was. All at once, a huge breaker came up out of nowhere and sloshed over him, soaking his clothes.

Served him right. He went home and went to bed.

*   *   *

The next day, he had Olga drive him out to the Club Revolución. On the way, she asked him, What happened to the men in the Tarkovsky film? When they got to the room that would show them their deepest desire.

Oh, I guess you could say the movie copped out. They decided it was better not to know their deepest desires after all. They never opened the door.

Too bad. I would really like to have known what was on the other side of that door.

No you wouldn't.

*   *   *

At the Club, he again went swimming in the ocean, but today he could find no pleasure in it; nor could he enjoy the jacuzzi or the pool. He fired up a cigar, but tossed it away after a few drags.

He took a cab back to the apartment. After he showered, he tried to read a travel guide to Havana; to find someplace to eat, to hear music; anything to take his mind off himself. But the page went blank before his eyes.

A knock at his door.

Sr. Kaiser, may I talk to you? It was the señora. Oh God. She knew. She *knew.*

Kaiser bid her come in and prepared himself to receive what he deserved. Sra. Barranco had something in her hand. She was smiling.

You like Che Guevara, *sí?*

She pressed into his hand a silver coin, a three-peso piece. Che's picture, frowning and militant, was engraved upon it.

A reminder of Cuba, she said.

And of the worthlessness of Cuban pesos, better given as gifts than spent.

He thanked her and she left the room. Now he felt even worse.

He went to the closet, where he had placed the contraband books and videos. Despite what the woman had said, there had been no phone call. He had to make one more effort to find Lázaro Perdomo.

*   *   *

He had given Olga the rest of the day off, so he went out on the Malecon and flagged a taxi for the ride to Havana Centro. Once again, he found himself on pothole street, with those Detroit classics in the same position. He wished he'd brought chalk to mark the tires, just to see if they ever moved. Again the domino players next to the door, wearing the same clothes. And again up the narrow dusty stairs to the second floor; the wooden boards lying between the apartments, and he knocked.

Quién es?

Buscando Lázaro Perdomo, he said.

Oh yes. He was going to call you. He was in luck: the English-speaking woman was there. But the door remained closed.

He knows who you are. He said for you to bring the books and he would meet you at the entrance to the park across from the Cine Yara at eleven PM.

The Cine Yara. Next to the Habana Libre?

Sí.

The Cine Yara, he knew from the guide books, was the most notorious gay cruising ground in Havana. The park across from it was also the location of the opening and closing scenes of *Fresa y Chocolate*, the most celebrated Cuban film (and a film about gays).

On his way down the stairs, Kaiser passed a man in a maroon *guayabera* shirt. Kaiser didn't think anything of it at first, but an uncomfortable feeling made him turn around. Sure enough, the man had stopped at the floor above and was looking down at him. He was wearing the kind of oval sunglasses that cops all around the world seemed to wear, and the neat rectangular black mustache that so often accompanied it. He remembered what Silvio had said: the *guayabera* was the official uniform of the Ministry of the Interior, the secret police; at any public gathering, you looked around for the *guayabera* man. And this guy certainly looked the part. Undoubtedly, he was there checking up on this subversive, Lázaro Perdomo. Kaiser turned around and walked out of the building as quickly as he could without revealing his panic.

But perhaps the appointment with Perdomo was a less fearful prospect than sitting around reflecting upon his own behavior so far on this trip. Maybe that's why he was able to summon the courage to make the eleven PM rendezvous across the street from the Yara. In one hand he held the bag with the contraband tapes and videos. Behind him was the line for admittance to the famous ice cream café at the Parque Coppelia. The line was always long, and seemed never to move. People also milled about constantly, so you could never tell who was on line and who was simply hanging out. Maybe that was why it was such a pick-up spot, primarily for gays, but sometimes straights as well.

The night had gotten off to a bizarre start already. He had gotten a sandwich at a café at the bottom of La Rampa. Afterward, as he climbed the hill beside the Hotel Habana Libre, he heard what sounded like the hissing of some ferocious big cat. He looked into the ferns planted beside the hotel and saw a guy, a kid in his late teens, lying on the ground curled up on his side. He wore no clothes except for a pair of baggy shorts. The kid hissed again, showing his teeth. A sexual hustler of some kind, or just another Cuban loco?

Kaiser paced up and down and looked at his watch. He thought about that night in Tel Aviv when he had left his gay friend's house, and the shame he had felt. That shame was one reason he felt he had to be right here, right now.

A boney-faced black man in a Morissey T-shirt, with a long pony tail trailing from his Florida Marlins cap, came out of the shadows.

Buenas noches, he said with a smile.

Are you Lázaro Perdomo?

No. He shook his head. I just thought you might want to go to a party.

Gracias. Some other time, Kaiser said.

The fellow walked away in the direction of the Malecón. A few paces further down, Kaiser watched him strike up a conversation with a guy with a shaved head and multiple nose and lip piercings who was leaning against a tree.

Kaiser checked his watch again and turned his head back in the direction of the Habana Libre. There, crossing the street, eyes set upon Kaiser, was the man in the maroon *guayabera*. He was no longer wearing sunglasses, but otherwise he looked exactly as he had earlier in the day, with the same stern expression.

Kaiser's first impulse was to throw the bag of books into the park shrubs and run. But that was pointless; the man would clearly see him do it. He saw that the black guy who had spoken to him before had apparently found the man by the tree receptive. The two were walking toward the end of the block. Kaiser went running after them. He caught up just as they were about to swing around the corner.

Hey, he said breathlessly. That party invitation still open?

Por qué no? the guy in the baseball hat said. He pointed to a Lada parked a couple of paces ahead of them. The two gay men got in the front seat while Kaiser jumped in back, still carrying his bag of books.

Kaiser was hoping the guys were heading west toward Miramar; that way they could let him out at his apartment near the Cohiba Hotel. Instead, they appeared to be headed east. The next thing he knew, they were going through the long tunnel that led away from the city, toward Guanabacoa and the eastern beaches. The two gays were swapping jokes and gossip between giggles, and they had pretty much forgotten the guy in the back seat.

They turned off the main road. It was dark, but there was enough moonlight that Kaiser could tell they were in a poor people's *barrio*, not unlike some districts he remembered from Alabama. The houses were just huts with wild palms between them and goats and chickens behind. Kaiser got a bit nervous remembering stories of tourists robbed in Cuba, but he relaxed when he saw they were headed for a big structure with lights on and cars parked in front.

The destination appeared to be a café or recreational center with a simple concrete apartment complex on either side of it. Exactly the place for a high school dance. A gray-haired lady at a folding table in front of the door was selling tickets just like for a church social. Through the many open windows, he could see a crowd of people milling about, and he could hear dance music loud over the PA.

Kaiser and his two companions got out of the car. Kaiser offered the driver a five-dollar bill for the ride, but the man declined.

Thanks, Kaiser said. Your name is . . .

Felix.

Well, listen Felix: turns out I'm not feeling so good. I think I'd like to go back to town. Where can I get a taxi?

You'd have to walk all the way back to the main road. There will be many taxis here when the show is over. Why don't you just go in and enjoy the performance?

Kaiser sighed and walked toward the building with the two men.

We built this whole complex with our own labor, Felix said. The people of this neighborhood. What have you got in that bag?

Books and videos. They were for a man I was supposed to meet. But he never showed.

Kaiser got at the end of the ticket line, but Felix and his friend kept walking.

Hey, Kaiser asked. Aren't you going in?

Of course, *mi amor*. But I use the performer's entrance. Then he and his friend disappeared around the side of the building.

Kaiser purchased a ticket and went inside. The place was ordinarily a cafeteria, which in Cuba simply means any informal restaurant, but the kitchen, behind swinging doors, was dark tonight, and the middle of the floor had been cleared for dancing. The tables had been pulled into a ring around this space. A makeshift stage had been created at the far end of the room. The curtains appeared to have been made from bed sheets. In the middle of the rear wall behind the stage was a benignly smiling picture of Che.

The audience seemed to be evenly divided between the most extreme kinds of urban bizarros: gender benders with punk hairdos and piercings, and their opposite number, older people of the most traditional sort, whom the Cubans call *guajiros*—country folks is about the closest one can come in translation. It wasn't until he got home and read his travel guide that Kaiser was to learn how this odd human conjunction had come to pass: this neighborhood, La Malandanza, was originally a place where itinerants took refuge on the outskirts of Havana: bohemians, the mentally ill, gays, Santeria sorcerers and other assorted eccentrics lived in makeshift houses. Later, they were joined by people who came in from rural regions looking for work.

Kaiser was still looking the place over when he was shocked to see, moving through the crowd, the maroon *guayabera*. And the shirt-owner's eyes were fixed directly on Kaiser. *Ay, Cuba!* He was good, this one. He must have followed Felix's car all the way out here. Fortunately, the man's progress was hindered by the crush of people.

Kaiser managed to squeeze around behind the stage, where a large storage room had a golden crepe star affixed to it. When a man walked out, Kaiser grabbed the door and held it open. The place had been converted into a dressing room. Felix and a number of others were getting ready for a show.

Felix?

Sí.

I'm in a bit of a bind. Someone that I don't want to see is looking for me. May I hide in here for a while?

Sure.

Kaiser edged into the crowded room.

We'll do even better, *mi cara*, Felix said. How would you like a foolproof disguise?

Sounds great.

No one will recognize you; I guarantee. You're going to get a complete makeover!

Everyone but Kaiser was laughing. He looked around the room and saw why: there were elaborate dresses on hangers, huge wigs on dummy heads, and a row of high-heeled shoes, toes against the wall. They were putting on a drag show tonight. He was surrounded by a roomful of queens at the midpoint of the transformation: their hair held down by netting to accommodate wigs, their lower torsos squeezed into body stockings, makeshift gaffs between their legs so genitalia wouldn't show.

Ernesto can't make it tonight, so you can take his place. Felix pushed Kaiser into a chair, and borrowed a safety razor from a huge man who had his foot up on a bench in order to shave his leg.

First, this has to go, Felix said, pointing to Kaiser's moustache and goatee. He wet the beard and rubbed it with soap; then he dispatched it with a few smooth strokes. Kaiser wasn't happy about losing the beard that he had begun growing on his first trip to Cuba, but the whole evening had so disoriented him that he had by this point become fatalistic. Powerful but invisible forces seemed to be buffeting him about. What next?

Felix was applying make-up. He shadowed Kaiser's eyes with some purple compound that smelled awful. Then came false eyelashes. Kaiser recognized them as made from the common carbon paper found in an office.

In Cuba, you must learn to improvise, said Felix.

They wanted to affix long red fingernails to his fingers with glue that had come from a shoe factory, but Kaiser demurred and instead was given long nightclub-vamp gloves, which turned out to be ordinary rubber household work gloves with sunbursts of cheap sequins pasted on the back. Earrings had been crafted from the caps of soda bottles. A red dress was brought for him to wear: it was given a ruffled effect by plastic garbage bags crumpled under a layer of cloth. The white feathers of the collar were in fact shreds of toilet paper.

Sometimes TP is harder to get in Cuba than the real feathers! Felix joked.

Then the wig: Kaiser now had an orange-blonde Afro. He balked at the high heels. Having never learned to walk in them, he would break his neck. Especially since he had been all this taking time taking hits off a bottle of raw-but-righteous *aguardiente* that was being passed around the room

Felix brought Kaiser a mirror.

Construimos El Hombre Nuevo! he giggled.

Kaiser thought himself not particularly pretty, but probably unrecognizable. Whatever male gender-terror he might have felt at the sight of himself as a woman was overwhelmed by his relief at the success of the disguise. Kaiser folded up his man-clothes and stuck them in the same bag with the contraband books and films.

Felix took him over to where a set of small figures were arranged upon an altar. Kaiser recognized them as the Orishas, the sacred entities of Santería. Every little figure wore the robe of his/her special color. There were offerings in front of each: rum, cigars, trinkets, food, money.

Give him a present, Felix said. He pointed at a red-robed figure.

Shangó, Kaiser said.

Ah . . . you know a little bit, Felix said. Kaiser did know that Shangó, the Orisha of sex, wore red and white. He found the jeans he had abandoned in order to put on his costume, fished out the three-peso piece that Sra. Barranco had given him and tossed it into the dish.

Shangó likes American money best, Felix suggested.

Kaiser pulled out a five dollar bill and put that in the dish. Kaiser realized that he was wearing Shangó's colors, red and white. Each performer was related to an Orisha in that way. Elegguá wears red and black, Oshún is yellow, Ogun black and green, Babalú Ayé (of Desi Arnaz fame) purple, and so on.

You know the story of Shangó and Ogun? Shangó fought with Ogun, the ruler of war. Shangó was defeated, but he managed to escape through the forest by diguising himself as a woman.

That sounded good to Kaiser.

I guess I'll just hide back here until the party's over, Kaiser said.

What do you mean, Felix said. You go on in ten minutes. You have to take Ernesto's place.

What? That's crazy. I don't have anything to perform.

Don't worry. It's like karaoke, but you don't even sing; you just mime the song as it's played. I've written down the words. Just move your lips; you'll be fine.

Kaiser was too stunned to offer any resistance. To ensure that he remained stunned, Felix gave him the remainder of the bottle of *aguardiente* and guided him out of the dressing room to the wings of the stage. One of the queens was at the microphone, speaking to the audience. He couldn't understand every word that she said, but it was clear that she was dedicating this performance to the glory of the revolution. She waved at the poster of Che behind the stage:

Construimos El Hombre Nuevo! she shouted. The crowd applauded.

Then she went into her number. Recorded music crackled out from old speakers. Wearing a tight black dress, she slunk forward and bared her white teeth. She began to mime the words to the song that a female voice sang on the recording. Felix translated for Kaiser:

> *I'm half-tiger and half-songbird*
> *Don't try to trick me*
> *You've seen the beautiful bird of paradise*
> *Try to put me in a cage and you'll see the fangs!*

And she raised her hands, hands in long black gloves that rose to the elbow, and clawed the air. Strange: dressing as a woman had put this man in touch not with feminine gentleness but with his/her aggression.

Same with the next performer, the huge man with the pony tail who had been shaving his legs a few minutes earlier. He began mouthing a song from another recording, and again rage was the emotion, the enormous man, six-and-a-half feet tall, shaking a hammy fist adorned with turquoise rings and silver bracelets as he raged against man, men, God, nature, society.

Then came a sketch with props. This queen had taken the role of a homeless woman, a Cuban bag lady. The stage was made to look like an alley with impromptu clotheslines strung across it; the woman's possessions were in a pile next to her and trash was scattered in front. She wore a torn blouse, a skirt formed from a bath towel, and laceless men's work boots whose tongues wagged as she walked. She was a mad woman, she sang. People mocked her and called her *la loca*. They didn't want to know what she had been: factory worker, soldier, whore, wife, mother; she had been all these. She had been brought to this state by passion and the cruelty of men. She shook her trembling hands in front of her face.

You're next! Felix said. He handed Kaiser a paper with the song lyrics he was supposed to mime in Spanish; he had thoughtfully written an English translation above them so that Kaiser would understand what he was saying. He no longer felt frightened. Was he in touch with the power of Shangó, or was it just some mighty strong *aguardiente*? He knew that in Santería, the Orishas are not gods or transcendent beings, but forces within the human psyche. In the ceremonies, you didn't invoke these spirits; nor did you become possessed by them. You became them. And it was fascinating that in most of the their songs, the performers were not expressing the rage of oppressed gay men, or of drag queens, but instead speaking as actual *women*. He read the lyrics Felix had given him:

> *You'll never know what it's like to be a woman*
> *Men are vain and false*
> *Wait, you just wait.*
> *You'll end up alone like me*

Suddenly, Felix shouted: *Lázaro*!

Kaiser looked around.

Lázaro finalmente!

Backstage, Felix was talking to an old man—or a man made up to look old. He had artificially grayed hair, a work shirt dyed purple from which the sleeves had been torn off at the seams, and a pair of dirty trousers with worn out knees. A small skinny brown dog was tied to a leash that went through an unbelted loop of his pants. There was a crutch carved from a forked tree branch under his right shoulder. Kaiser recognized the Santería figure of Babalú-Ayé, yes, the one Ricky Ricardo sang about on *I Love Lucy*—the Orisha, who, as Kaiser had learned, represented sickness/ healing and resurrection. The only unusual note was that this Babalú-Ayé was in high heels like those Kaiser had recently refused. Kaiser couldn't fully understand the conversation, but he seemed to be apologizing to Felix for being late.

You are Lázaro? Kaiser asked.

Sí. Don't I look like Lázaro?

You've got to get out of here.

Me? But why?

There's a man from MININT outside in the audience. I though he was after me, but now I realize he only wanted me to lead him to you. You're in trouble! And I am, too, probably.

You're sure?

We'll go out the back way. I'll tell you more then.

He can't leave! said Felix. We have our sketch to do in fifteen minutes. You're in it, too.

Kaiser grabbed the bag with the books—and now, his clothes as well. He went to the back door and stuck his head out.

Come on!

Lázaro followed, tossing aside his crutch.

Ay Cuba! Felix howled.

Out behind the building was a stretch of vegetation where the jungle squatted and plotted to reclaim the town. Stepping through waist-high foliage in a full-length dress was quite a chore. Next time I do this, he vowed, I'll wear a mini-skirt. And he thanked Shangó that he had not put on high heels, though Lázaro seemed to be managing well in his.

Kaiser stepped on something long and narrow that he took to be the root of a tree until it moved beneath his foot. Kaiser jumped, sure he'd stepped on a very big snake. But then he heard a whispered voice:

Hijo de puta!

He had stomped on someone's arm. The woods around him, he now realized were full of soft human voices, not speaking but making the sounds of love. Lázaro's puppy yipped softly; you could hear the rope that connected him to his master slipping like a snake through the high weeds. Kaiser stopped and leaned against a palm.

Lázaro smiled at him.

I got to say, this is the most unusual pitch I've ever gotten,he said.

No. I wasn't kidding, said Kaiser. I'm the guy you told to meet you at Cine Yara.

I did?

And there's a cop back there who's been looking for you for days.

What on earth for?

You'd know better than me. One reason is these books in my bag. They're from Ricardo in Los Angeles.

In *Estados Unidos*?

Of course.

I don't know any Ricardo in Los Angeles. I don't know anyone in Los Angeles.

Aren't you Lázaro Perdomo?

Lázaro Perdomo? *Quien es?*

But Felix called you Lázaro.

I'm the character Lázaro in his show. My real name is Rodolfo.

But you're dressed like Babalú-Ayé.

Sí. San Lázaro.

Kaiser finally understood. He remembered again that all Orishas had the names of Christian saints in order to hide their African origin. Shangó was Santa Barbara. And Babalú-Ayé was indeed San Lázaro. Lazarus the risen from the dead. Kaiser had the wrong guy.

That means, he said, that the cop is after me, not you. I can't go back to the club.

So this is not a pitch.

No. I'm sorry.

Don't be. I was going to tell you that drag queens don't interest me.

He winked and smiled.

You can stay at my house, Rodolfo said, if you don't mind sleeping in the bed with my kids. I would let you sleep in my bed, he chuckled, but my wife doesn't like it. You know, she says, *Whatever you do outside is your business but in this house ya-ya-ya.* I'll take you there and go back to the club. Felix is probably having an absolute fit; I mean, bouncing off the walls.

Come on, Chucho, he said, and tugged gently on the puppy's rope. Kaiser followed him into the village. Many of the houses were like the classic Cuban huts, *bohios*, but they sported metal roofs rather than the traditional thatch. Rodolfo, however, had one of the standard little square post-revolution concrete cottages of which Kaiser had seen many: a kitchen, a parlor and two bedrooms. The first was the kids' room: there were four of them, Kaiser could see, lying on two mattresses. Rodolfo went in and woke the two oldest, telling them there was company.

Kaiser put his bag down and took out his man-clothes. He took off the dress and gloves. He put on his jeans and shirt, knelt down and squeezed himself in between kid three and kid four. The kids stirred briefly and parted to let him in. A bit later he heard Rodolfo return, and a few minutes later, he heard moans from the next room: Rodolfo was putting the cap on a busy night by fulfilling his marital duty with his wife.

*　　*　　*

Madrugada. Kaiser loved the sound of that word. He rose with the first rays of morning light. Moving carefully and quietly, he put on his shoes and found the house's small bathroom. He realized he still had make-up on his face, so he washed it off, keeping the faucet only slightly open so as not to make noise. Then he tip-toed to the front door.

He remembered the bag, still in the kids' room. He momentarily considered leaving it for Rodolfo, who would probably enjoy the contents, but there was still a chance that the elusive Perdomo might contact him. There was now a hole torn in one side of the bag, so Kaiser had to carry it in his arms like a baby rather than by its handles. He was startled when he thought he saw two snakes copulating in the road ahead of him, but it turned out to be only a tree branch, which he kicked aside. By the time he reached the main road, it was full daylight. His strategy was to walk in the direction of Havana until he came to a bus stop.

On the other side of the road, he saw a parked Mercedes, a government car, with a man slouching in the front seat. As Kaiser went past, the man stirred and turned on his engine. Then Kaiser heard the car make a fast U in the middle of the deserted road. A second later, it pulled up beside him. The driver flung open the passenger door. Kaiser leaned to enter and was about to thank the driver, when he recognized the man. It was the *guayabera.*

Well, shit. No point in resisting; they were on to him and undoubtedly knew everything. He climbed wearily into the car.

Buenos días, he said. You been sitting here all this time?

The man nodded. He spoke good English. There's only one road, he said. You had to come out sooner or later.

The cop had waited, as Olga had been prepared to wait for hours for him in her car as part of her duty. In Cuba, people had learned how to wait.

You have the books and films?

Kaiser sighed and nodded, handing him the bag. The man looked through the contents.

Excellent, excellent, he said with relish.

Apparently, this was a really nice bust for him. Maybe he'd get a promotion. The man put the bag in the back seat and started the car again.

Kaiser was resigned as they drove toward the city. There would be a long and unpleasant session of questioning coming, but if he was lucky, he would only be deported.

So Ricardo gave you these?

That's right. Kaiser had decided to answer all questions truthfully in the hope of leniency.

Delightful boy, Ricardo. Absolutely delightful. And the second *delightful* was spoken with an unmistakable tinge of gay-male lasciviousness that startled Kaiser.

Wait a minute, Kaiser said. You know him personally?

But of course. I am Lázaro Perdomo.

Relief poured thick like honey through Kaiser's nerves.

Good God. Because of the shirt, I thought you were with the Ministry of the Interior.

That too. Yes, I work for the MININT.

Kaiser was for once in his life speechless.

Don't look so shocked. In every country, intelligence agencies are full of gays. When you think about it, it makes sense. What was your guy's name? J. Edward Hoover?

Close enough.

Now Kaiser understood why the neighbors had looked uncomfortable when he mentioned the name Lázaro Perdomo. Not because Perdomo was in trouble with the cops. Because he *was* a cop.

So who did I speak to at your apartment? Kaiser asked.

My wife and daughter. I don't live there any more. After thirty years, my wife said *Bastante*! and told me to find another house. She has a lover and she wants to marry him. I can't say I blame her. She deserves more than a marriage of convenience. But in those days, it was necessary to keep up appearances.

So has it really changed in Cuba? For gays, I mean.

It's better. You still have to walk softly, but that's true anywhere, eh?

They stopped at the highway checkpoint for cars going into Havana. It looked like a big toll gate. This guy was MININT, all right: when a guard came up to the window, Lázaro Perdomo flashed something in his wallet at him, and the man straightened up and nodded nervously, then waved them through.

Where are you staying? I'll drop you off.

Vedado.

They entered the tunnel back to Havana.

I'm so grateful, said the cop. I love to read, you know, and it's very difficult to get books here, even the ones that aren't controversial. Don't get me wrong: I still believe in the Revolution. The young who criticize it don't know what it was like here before. So you live in Los Angeles?

For the last twenty-five years or so, yes.

Ricardo wants to be in the movies. Do you work in films?

Not any more. I used to be a screenwriter, though.

They exited the tunnel and began winding along the Malecón. The sun was bright today, but high waves were still splashing over the sea wall.

Really! said the MININT man. The policeman was excited. Do you have an agent?

No. He dropped dead suddenly a couple of years ago. Kind of gave a nice closure to my Hollywood experience.

Someday I want to write a screenplay, Lázaro Perdomo said. It can't be done under the current circumstances, of course. But I can wait. *He* can't live forever.

There seems to be some debate about that.

The stories I could tell you. I've got all the good dirt on the big-wigs. And not just the Cubans. I mean all the foreign dignitaries that come here, and the famous authors, and the celebrities—

Kaiser cut him off. If you want to know the truth, I think your own story would be far more interesting.

How do you mean?

The conflict between your job and your true self. During that time when homosexuality was forbidden as counterrevolutionary.

There was a long pause. To Kaiser's discomfort, the cop chose to draw an inference.

You think I'm a hypocrite, don't you? That's what you mean, isn't it?

I didn't say that.

But it's what you think. Admit it; you think I'm a hypocrite.

Kaiser was groping for a way out of this.

I think I mean that you must have felt like a divided person. That's not the same as being a hypocrite . . . especially in Cuba. Everything here is all mixed up and turned around.

Not like in your country, eh?

Kaiser remained silent.

They had reached Kaiser's apartment building in Vedado. Kaiser thanked Lázaro Perdomo as he got out.

Are you doing anything tonight? he asked as Kaiser got out of the car. I can show you some very exciting out-of-the-way places.

I bet you can, said Kaiser, but tonight I have to fly back to Tijuana. In a few hours, I'll be on the red-eye.

When he reached the apartment and knocked, Sra. Barranco opened the door, a robe over her nightgown. She smiled when she saw him, and he could tell she was fighting to keep from giggling. He thought that was odd. People don't usually giggle when you wake them early in the morning.

It wasn't until he went into his room and looked in the mirror that he understood. He was still wearing his bottle-cap earrings.

XVI

Kaiser slept most of the day; then it was time to pack for the flight home. He ate dinner at a good paladar in the neighborhood; then he settled up the bill with Sra. Barranco. Cecilia was nowhere around, so he didn't see or speak to her before his departure. But Mrs. Barranco seemed quite pleased with him as a guest; he didn't sense that she was hiding any animosity.

The home flight left at four in the morning; to avoid disturbing the sleeping Barrancos, he took a taxi to the airport several hours early. There was no waiting room at the small terminal; he had to sit outside by a coffee kiosk and smoke cigars until the time came for him to check in. Then it was through the little booth for passport control. Momentarily, he was anxious: he'd undergone that lengthy search at this point in his last visit. But this time he went through without incident and a little later he was on the plane.

*   *   *

The trip to TJ was hell, as always. For some awful reason, all passengers had to disembark in Monterey in order to get their passports stamped. This made it impossible to sleep through the flight. When they arrived in Tijuana, it was eight in the morning and he was feeling the acute pain of unrelieved wakefulness. He took a cab to the Grand Hotel, where he had made a reservation for early arrival. They gave him a room high up, overlooking a golf course. He fell into a dreamless sleep for eight hours.

When he awoke, it was early evening. A talk show was on MTV: a young man said he compensated for the lack of sensation produced by wearing a condom by thinking of the condom as some sort of kinky sex toy. Worth a try, Kaiser thought.

Kaiser got dinner in the restaurant on the first floor; then he took a cab to the border. He crossed on foot, found his car, paid his bill and drove back into Mexico. He would park in the hotel's underground lot, then drive back into the USA in the morning.

But when he got to La Revo at the top of the hill, he turned right, not left, and parked in the big lot right by the taco stand. What the hell. He wanted to top off the trip with a pit stop at the Frontera.

So there he was, one more time, heading downhill from Revolución, through the pleasant chaos of the Zona Norte. It was too early for the Frontera to be really busy, but there were plenty of girls. He fancied one woman on a stool by the bar. She had on a black dress, and her dark hair was gathered in an old-fashioned bun, held with a rhinestone-studded plastic comb. When he approached, her eyes got big. She was appealingly shy. As they walked upstairs, he asked her name.

Victoria, she said, but not Victoria's Secret, and she giggled.

When they got to the room, she flipped off the pink dress and her high heels. She wore a gold bracelet around her ankle. Her body was lithe: thin, but soft in the right places. She sat beside him on the bed; he put his arm around her. She gave out a little peep when he bit one of her nipples a trifle too hard; he had to tell her that he wasn't going to hurt her and reassure her with a hug.

When he lay on his back, she jumped astride him and got up on her toes like a dancer, wriggling until she found an angle at which he could feel her contract around him. Then in a series of quick, jumping strokes, she brought him off.

Victoria indeed. He could still come inside a woman, even with a thick condom on. All it took, really, was a bit of fiddling around to find a point where there was friction. The problem was that the women he'd been with in the last year had either been waiting for him to give them instructions, or else were paying him no attention at all.

Afterward, they talked for a while. She spoke good English. She was from the D.F. She had two kids. She had worked with computers. She was saving up money to open a computer store on *el otro lado*, in the US. She even knew the place she wanted: a storefront near the Chula Vista off-ramp on the 405.

She invited him to join her in the shower, and he did. Beneath the warm waters, he put his arm around her and kissed her cheek. He said he would like to see her again, and she said she would be there the next Saturday at the same time. They left the room holding hands. As they passed the desk, the man with the gray mustache said something in Spanish that Kaiser didn't catch.

Did you hear what he said to me? she asked.

No.

He said, You look happy.

No kidding? That's great!

He kissed her goodbye.

*   *   *

Sunday he slept all day. He woke up still tired Monday morning and put on the conservative blazer and tie that his lawyer had recommended. As he drove to the courthouse, he was still thinking about Cuba and Tijuana and not about the fact that he was about to go on trial for what amounted to his life. This was all to the good, he figured, because more anxiety at this point would only be counterproductive.

Valdevaria met him in the courthouse cafeteria, and over coffee she advised him what was in store. The jury selection would take some time; it was unlikely the trial proper would start today. Tuesday would be an off day because Kaiser had requested it in order to accommodate his teaching schedule. Wednesday would be Showtime.

The courtroom was high on the top floor of the courthouse. The judge, Malvina Sykes, was a wiry black woman with big glasses and a somber demeanor. Valdevaria had had her before and said she could be tough.

Tough but fair? Kaiser ventured hopefully.

Tough, the lawyer replied.

Tulsky was on hand again, with McGinnis beside him. They were soon joined by Veronica, who was careful not to look at Kaiser as she entered and took her seat. She was wearing a suit, unusual for a woman so young. It looked brand new. Probably purchased with some of the bonanza from the settlement with the college. Except for the brown color, it was the twin of a gray one worn by Virginia McGinnis, confirming Kaiser's suspicion that the older woman was Veronica's mentor.

His own lawyer was the pickier of the two during the selection process, but Tulsky made plenty of challenges as well, and eventually most of the alternates were called. After a while, Kaiser began to get the gist of his attorney's strategy. She was bumping the people whom Kaiser would have normally considered to be most sympathetic to him: a hippie gardener was bounced, as was a lesbian chef, a black female postal employee and, most tellingly, a middle-aged woman who was a part-time English instructor at a community college. On the other hand, a tattooed biker, a female church choir director, a gun shop owner and a retired Marine officer suited Teresa Valdevaria just fine.

Everything in this country is all mixed up, all confused, Kaiser thought as the day's proceedings ended.

*   *   *

So what do you think of Florentino now, eh? he asked the class. He's had six hundred twenty-two love affairs. He's acted out every conceivable fantasy. The only principle that limited his behavior was that he refused to pay for love with money.

Didn't he break that rule?

You're right, Cleon. He finally met a woman whose resolve was as strong as his own in that regard. She believed that love should always be paid for. How'd that work out?

She gets him to agree to pay, but only one peso.

A symbolic fee. What about some of his other affairs? They take him into some scary places, don't they? The woman with the pigeons gets killed because of him, doesn't she? Her husband cuts her throat because Florentino's carelessness revealed the affair. But weren't some of his affairs even more disturbing?

A hand went up.

Yes, Tranh.

The young girl. His niece.

What happened?

She was fifteen years old. She's his own niece and he is supposed to be her guardian and protector. Instead, he has sex with her. And he doesn't realize how deeply she's been affected by all this. So he knows he's responsible when she commits suicide later.

What's her name, Tranh?

America Vicuña.

Significance of that name? Anybody? Well, a vicuña is a type of llama that has especially fine wool. It's very expensive material. They're very small and delicate animals. Okay. Now he makes two shocking discoveries at this point doesn't he? One is what he's done to the girl. The other is . . . yes, Sonia.

He's deforested the river. The trees have all been chopped down for firewood for his company's boats. He never noticed before because he never went on the river because he was all preoccupied with his love life in the city.

So he did to the land—America—what he did to the girl. Of course, he loved the girl. He also loved the river. But García Márquez is showing us the dark side of this sentimental romanticism that the Europeans brought to what we now call third-world countries. Remember a few weeks ago we read what Zadie Smith said: how the English really did love India just as they claimed, and that this was the problem: *People treat their lovers badly.*

Pause.

But what does García Márquez think of Florentino? I think we could say the book has a happy ending. Florentino gets what he's always wanted. Does Florentino deserve such forgiveness? What is our judgment of him? Yes, Ziaou Zie?

I don't know why you're so preoccupied with judging these characters. Isn't a great writer like García Márquez supposed to look upon his characters as though they were living beings, without judging them?

Kaiser nodded. I've heard that adage, too: that a great author doesn't judge his or her characters. But I don't think I buy it. In fact, we are always making judgments about the people we encounter, in real life or in fiction, and authors, even great ones, are no different than the rest of us. So I ask you again, knowing now what he did to his fifteen-year-old niece, what he did to the river . . . what is your judgment on Florentino?

Kaiser looked out over the group and noted for the first time that the veiled Aisha was not in attendance today. The class remained silent.

Well?

*　　*　　*

Game day.

Kaiser had been unable to eat breakfast. As they awaited the arrival of the judge in the courtroom, he played with his tie. He had chosen a standard regimental, not too wide, as his attorney had requested.

Periodically, he glanced at Veronica Tafuliya sitting at the plaintiff's table. Whereas two days earlier she'd seemed taciturn and sour like her mentor McGinnis, now she was altogether different: elated, excited, turning one way, then another to ask her attorneys a question, stealing quick glances at supporters in the gallery; she was like a birthday girl; all she needed was to be surrounded by helium balloons, with curled confetti streamers hanging from the ceiling. It was a coming-out party for the little immigrant waif, her true arrival in America. She had been accepted into the mechanism of power. She was the center of attention. And she was smiling; smiling broadly so that all the metal work flashed like a searchlight at a Hollywood premiere.

Judge Sykes entered and everybody rose. She gaveled the proceedings to order, and seemed to be in a salty mood. After the usual rituals, opening statements were made. Tulsky was the more emotional. He was going to show them how this sleazebag teacher had abused his position of trust and similarly abused his client. Valdevaria was brief and to the point: the plaintiffs case was all unsubstantiated charges and innuendo without a shred of real evidence.

Tulsky went for Kaiser right away, calling him to the stand immediately. Kaiser had the feeling that Tulsky thought they were going to make him look so bad that he and McGinnis wouldn't even have to present the rest of the case; so bad that Kaiser would be begging for a settlement by lunchtime.

Once he took the stand, Kaiser looked at the gallery and saw that Dean James of Academic Affairs was there, along with Lucy Kronsky, his department head, and Dr. Cardona, the campus Disciplinarian. In fact, every personage of authority that he'd dealt with since this whole sorry affair started had managed to clear time for this show. And there were students as well; he recognized a couple of the campus women's group leaders who had demanded his resignation, as well as a reporter for the student newspaper the *Roller* who had tried to interview him while he was walking across the quad a few months back. Kaiser had just kept saying No comment, enjoying feeling like a renegade corporate exec for a few minutes.

Tulsky was again handling the cross. Kaiser now understood the logic of this: just as it was good strategy for him to be represented by a woman, so it was likewise clever for his opponents to have him crucified by a man. It was a way of saying to the jury: *Hey, this was not just a guy doing the things guys do. Most men don't behave like this or approve of this behavior in other men.*

And Tulsky started down the list, the list of accusations designed as questions that Kaiser had first heard in the deposition, starting with his relationships (or lack of same) with women. His lawyer objected to the form of the question. Judge Sykes overruled her. When she objected again a moment later, the judge rebuked her:

Counselor, I think I made myself quite clear on this and the subsequent material prior to this hearing. If you continue to object, I will find you in contempt.

In other words, all the loony stuff from the deposition was to be allowed in. Valdevaria wasn't even going to be able to pull the old lawyer trick of objecting to slow down the momentum of the opposition's case.

So Tulsky began again with the questions about Cuba, about sexual tourism. There was the tape of his class where he talked about Cuba and its very friendly people. Then, of course, came the paper with the obscene graffiti at the end.

Will you read this out loud, Mr. Kaiser?

TURKS ARE LIVING PROOF THAT JEWS FUCK CAMELS, he said once more, and he again did what he had vowed not to do, steeled himself not to do, bit his lip to avoid doing:

He laughed.

Not a full-out guffaw, mind you, his jaw was clenched much too tightly for that. But a snort and a strangled chuckle were audible enough to be recognized for what they were. Tulsky was on it in a greedy millisecond.

You find this amusing, Mr. Kaiser?

It's just so absurd.

But there was no way to fix it now. Nor was there any way to fix it when Tulsky asked him about the underwear, the ass-grabbing, the peeing in bottles. Despite his denial of every fabrication, the damage was done simply by being asked those questions in the first place. To be forced to deny them was demeaning in itself. And he thought he could tell why Judge Sykes had allowed all of it in court: she was poised above him with hungry eyes, circling around the carrion. This was the kind of thing that made her job fun: watching him squirm and try to answer one outrageous allegation after another was her idea of entertainment.

But Kaiser had been prepared for everything up to this point. He wasn't prepared for what came next. Tulsky began playing another tape, one that had been submitted as evidence but was never used at the deposition. Kaiser recognized it as the day of the last class, the one after which he had confronted Veronica in the hall about the harassment charges. She had taped him while they spoke. It was the time he had told her she was *so fuckin' ugly*. Not until it was played did he realize the full significance of his actual words: *No one will ever believe you because you're so fuckin' ugly*. What he hadn't considered was how those words would sound played aloud in court. They sounded like a boast about getting away with a crime: I did it, but no one will ever believe you.

And the final words: *so fuckin' ugly*. Kaiser could feel everyone in the courtroom wincing. It was hitting below the belt. It was like saying to a woman, any woman: I'm going to take the historical injustice that's been done to you (that women's looks matter so much) and use it against you. I'm a bully. I'm a sadist. I have no shame.

He had been most effectively demonized. He could feel a wave of rage pass through the courtroom. He was waiting to see if his even more shameful subsequent words would be coming next: *Tell your father he has lousy taste in women*—but the tape went blank, hissing and crackling. It had been erased. So he had discovered at last a point beyond which even Veronica wouldn't go.

Is that your voice, Mr. Kaiser?

Yes. But my words have to be understood in context.

Tittering was heard in the gallery. The judge had to gavel for silence.

Tulsky was clearly pleased. The sarcastic tone of his voice captured well the mood in the room.

And exactly what context is that, Mr. Kaiser?

This was the moment. He had to say it now. But conscience trapped the words in his chest before he could speak. He could say it, but did he have the *right* to say it? Had he earned the *right*?

The context is . . .

Yes?

The reason that I find her unattractive is . . .

Go ahead, Mr. Kaiser. We're all ears.

The context of the remark is that she's not really unattractive, but I find her unattractive only because . . .

Amazing how difficult it was to say it, even after everything he'd been through.

Because I . . .

(*Say it, say it!*)

It was only the smugness of Tulsky's self-satisfied grin that finally forced it out of him.

The context is that . . .

And it was as if his mouth was all rubbery from dentist's novocaine, and he struggled to get his lips around the words:

. . . that I am a homosexual.

The words came out as something between a grunt and a mumble.

I'm sorry, Tulsky said, frowning, Could you speak up?

But now Kaiser felt imbued with Shangó/Dennis Rodman boldness and insolence.

I said, I—AM—A—HOMOSEXUAL.

There; it was done.

I didn't mean that Veronica is really ugly. I meant that I found her unattractive because women don't interest me sexually.

I see. May I remind you that you're under oath?

Unh-huh.

Is this a recent discovery, Mr. Kaiser? Did you just realize it this morning?

I have always been what I am.

Well then, perhaps you could supply the court with the names of some of the men with whom you've had sex recently.

Sure. Bill. Ernie. DeAndre. Kaspar.

You can't give any full names?

I can do better than give you a name. There are two men in the courtroom now who will vouch for me.

He nodded in the direction of the gallery. On a back row sat Rich Goines and his friend Ricardo. Kaiser had cashed in the favor that Goines had promised him in return for delivering the books in Cuba. They had spoken on the phone the night before, and Rich Goines had suggested the ploy. He felt Kaiser deserved something more meaningful than Starbuck's gift certificates.

They'll vouch for you?

They will acknowledge that I've had sex with them, Kaiser clarified.

Tulsky was flustered. He walked back to McGinnis at the desk and spoke with her briefly. Then he turned to face the judge.

Your honor, we'd like to request a recess in order to discuss these developments.

Trumps were on the table.

He walked toward the parking structure beside Teresa Valdevaria. She was smiling.

I smell a settlement offer coming, she said. A nice one.

She stopped walking at the elevator.

Why didn't you tell me you were gay right from the start, Jack? It would have saved us so much trouble.

Oh, you know . . . it still bothers a lot of people. My family doesn't know, for one thing . . .

She just looked at him until her elevator arrived.

Of course, during the deposition, I was never asked directly or indirectly. I didn't know if it was appropriate or not . . .

She got in the elevator and turned to look at him, but her brow was just a little curly with suspicion.

*   *   *

He was confident he had calculated rightly. Tulsky could have argued that Kaiser was bisexual, but within the kingdom of current popular prejudice (which was the realm where trial juries lived) nobody, straight or gay, seemed to believe that bisexuals actually existed. Similarly, most people still believed instinctively that no straight male would be capable of declaring himself publicly to be gay, even to gain advantage.

He knew there was every possibility that Tulsky and McGinnis hadn't believed he was gay for a second. And that an effective cross might have poked holes in his story. But he reckoned that they surely had doubts about the veracity of their own client, and here Kaiser had served notice that he was ready to play the same game: to say anything, absolutely anything that was necessary. This was going to be a lot of work, and that would bring them to see Kaiser's final weapon: they had already, in the settlement from the school, gotten as much money as they were going to get out of this case. All that was really at stake now was the change in Veronica's grade from F back to A. It was time to declare victory and go home.

Of course, Kaiser was now guilty of perjury. But so was his adversary. It wasn't legal, but it was justice. That's all he had wanted. And where would Tulsky find evidence to refute the charge? Where would he find a woman who'd had sex with Kaiser in recent years? Not on this side of the border, that's for sure.

So he wasn't surprised when Teresa called around dinnertime.

Good news, Jack. They've made an offer, like I expected. They will drop the suit. They will pay all court costs. They will also pay any legal fees you have incurred. That means my bill.

Put a lot of expenses on it. Make sure they pay for all your meals.

Don't you worry. You also don't have to change the student's grade. It will remain an F.

Excellent.

You were concerned about vindication at work. They have agreed to submit a letter of apology which you can place in your file at school, as long as it stops short of saying they did anything wrong. All we have to do is waive the right to a counter-suit.

That's fine. I guess they'll get to keep their settlement money from the school, but that's not my problem. The college shouldn't have caved in so quickly. I got what I wanted.

She went on, The judge said she felt like levying a fine against Tulsky and McGinnis for bringing a frivolous lawsuit. When we went to her chambers, she said *You could tell that man was queer as a three-dollar bill just looking at him.*

Kaiser smiled.

We'll sign some papers next week. I'll let you know. And give me a call sometime and we'll have lunch.

It was the first such invitation she had extended to him. He was a little surprised, because he felt she suspected that he had lied. Maybe she wanted to satisfy her own curiosity on that point. Even so, he thought she was closer than ever to believing he was innocent. Not of perjury maybe, but innocent of *something*.

XVII

During the rest of the week, Kaiser observed a change in the atmosphere at school. The departmental secretary was friendly and solicitous, greeting him when he walked by the office. Lucy Kronsky passed through as he was checking his mail and gave him a thumbs-up with a big grin. When he walked down the corridor past the open doors of offices, the professors no longer looked away from him and pretended to be involved with work. Instead, they smiled and nodded. And when he clicked on his campus e-mail box, there were no anonymous messages calling him nasty names.

Kaiser thought only about getting back down to Tijuana and celebrating. He wanted to see Victoria again. He wanted to get to know her. He wanted to spend time with her, to learn about her. And he resolved to learn to speak Spanish, really speak it. You really didn't learn about a people, he now understood, unless you knew their language. Unless you knew the language and knew it well, you would always be disembodied, a ghost.

*　　*　　*

He reached TJ in the early afternoon, too early to go to the Frontera. He walked up and down Revolución and bought a couple of cigars. He passed a stall where some nice *guayaberas* were being sold; he picked out a green one with gold embroidery. When he got back to his motel, he tried it on, but he became anxious when he saw his reflection in the mirror and pulled it off. The figure in the glass looked far too much like Lázaro Perdomo.

When the sun went down, he ate a lobster at a seafood joint. Then he was headed on foot back to the Zona Norte, past the food stands, the musicians, the women working the street. Inside the Frontera, Kaiser took a seat at the bar, the one at the south end of the room.

He was waiting for Victoria. She wasn't around, but it was early yet.

The club filled to maybe two-thirds of capacity. Not like the old days when the stock market was booming, but still a decent crowd. There were plenty of girls, too: all the seats at the bar were occupied by girls, and some of them were very attractive.

He ordered several drinks so as to keep the bartender happy while he sat (and he accompanied each purchase with an extravagant tip), but after the first *cerveza*, he actually stopped drinking them. After two hours, though, no Victoria.

Finally, the barkeep spoke to him.

You looking for somebody special?

Is Victoria coming tonight?

Oh, Victoria. She's gone.

Gone where?

Back to the D.F. To her husband and kids. She made enough money to go back.

I see, said the blind man. Now Kaiser knew why she had looked so happy the week before. It had had nothing to do with him. She had made enough money to return home with a full *bolsa*, to go back to her family.

Determined not to fall into a funk of disappointment, he began looking around the room for another woman. He spied a familiar face way back at the corner table on the opposite side of the bar. There, with her feet up on a chair, sat Esmeralda, the girl he'd had on his first visit here. It seemed like longer, but it hadn't even been a year ago. She was wearing black slacks and a shiny new black leather jacket instead of a party dress. Her long black hair had been bobbed and she was looking off into space.

Buenas noches.

She smiled and nodded absently. She gave no sign of recognizing him, but he hadn't expected that she would.

Sixty? he asked. She nodded again.

Esmeralda? he asked her as they walked up the stairs. She nodded. She didn't ask him how he knew. She seemed more remote now. If this work had ever been an adventure for her, it had stopped being one long ago.

The room she took him to was different from the others he'd used here in only one respect. It was basically the same bare crib with only a bed and a mirror and a chair, except that over the head of the bed was a shelf with a working television on it. When he indicated that she should take the top, she motioned to him that he should lie with his head at the foot of the bed so that she could watch TV. The program was *El Gordo y La Flaca*, a talk show aimed at women that he sometimes watched in LA when he was trying to improve his Spanish. Today's guest was a famous Mexico City chef explaining how to prepare fish in a red *mole*.

After a few minutes, Kaiser told the woman to jump off. His old problem was back (where, oh where, was Victoria?) and he had her finish him up with her hand. Esmeralda continued to watch the TV show as she worked on him.

Finally, as he was putting his clothes back on, Kaiser asked: I've been with you before. *Tu me recuerdes*?

She didn't answer, just kept watching the show. Kaiser realized she hadn't spoken a word all night.

What's the matter? he asked. Have you lost your voice?

Sitting on the bed naked, she smiled, and her lips parted for the first time and Kaiser saw what she had been shyly hiding all this time: a dazzling, intricate set of new dental braces. Shiny as a row of freshly silvered mirrors, they seemed to fill the room with light.

*   *   *

Kaiser decided to drive back that night even though he had reserved a hotel room in Tijuana. He was in such a hurry to leave that he even forgot to remove, in case he was searched at the border, the bands that identified as Cuban the cigars he had purchased that afternoon. He also neglected to buy the obligatory bottle of tequila to wave at the border guard as his sole purchase in Mexico.

The agent at the border booth was a stout blond woman with a pony tail.

Purpose of your trip to Mexico? she asked.

I've been a bad boy, he answered. She was not amused, but she waved him on through.

He made a stop at the coffee kiosk on his way to San Diego. He knew it stayed open 'til the wee hours. The woman with the short blonde hair was there, but the blackboard with the quiz question was a *tabula rasa*.

No quiz?

People were cheating, the blonde woman said glumly.

From then on, he red-lined it back into LA. He had the alternative rock station on his radio. Leonard Cohen sang: *There's a war between the rich and poor, a war between the men and women / Why don' choo come on back to the war?*

He got home a little after three and went right to bed. He didn't sleep well. He couldn't stop seeing images of Esmeralda at the Frontera.

When he awakened Sunday morning, he realized that he hadn't checked his mailbox the night before when he arrived. In the box, he found a legal-sized envelope. Undoubtedly the settlement papers for him to sign. But when he actually spread the material out on the kitchen table, it appeared to be not a settlement at all, but a brand-new lawsuit brought against him by Veronica Tafuliya, now represented by a new lawyer named LaKeesha Habib.

It was afternoon now; late enough to call Teresa Valdevaria at home.

I thought we had a deal, he said.

We never signed the papers, but we had a verbal deal witnessed by the judge, which ordinarily is binding. But this is a new suit. Veronica is claiming she was defrauded. She claims she found a Paraguayan birth certificate that shows she actually turned eighteen two months ago, and that therefore her father had no right to make a settlement on her behalf. That he kept the knowledge from her in order to get his hands on the settlement money from the college. She's suing him to get that money back.

How does this relate to me?

She is claiming that there was a conspiracy to defraud her. You are named as her father's co-conspirator.

So Veronica had succeeded in making Kaiser identical with the hated father. Another nice piece of work.

Tulsky and McGinnis are also named as co-conspirators. She's trying to regain any fees paid to them, plus damages.

Kaiser almost chuckled. McGinnis had done a good job as mentor; now her protégé was going to show her how well she had been taught.

And yes, Valdevaria went on, I too am named as a defendant. I think she's going to claim we all knew about the Paraguayan birth certicate; that it was used as a bargaining chip in negotiations by her father and the lawyers.

So at least Kaiser would have Valdevaria to keep him company in this next phase.

She can't really do this, can she? Kaiser asked. We had a deal.

It's most unusual, the attorney said. But there are a couple of precedent cases.

It still wasn't over.

That night, he slept even less than the night before. Nothing he tried—brandy, yogic breathing, or a pill—could mollify his agitation. He managed to doze just a little before dawn when the morning sun—that sun that shines equally on the righteous and the wicked, as people are fond of saying, and leaves you to sort out in which camp you belonged—that sun stung his eyes into wakefulness. He understood that it wasn't really the new lawsuit that had caused his agitation.

He drove immediately to campus, even though he taught no classes on Mondays. He guzzled a coffee and went straight to the Admissions Office. He knew there were some eight-week classes that started mid-semester, right after spring vacation. He wanted to find out if there was a Spanish 1 section still open.

There was, the secretary informed him; in fact, there was a nine AM, right in the building next door. Kaiser took his enrollment slip from her, paid his fees at the cashier's window and got his receipt. Then he bought the Spanish textbook at the school store.

By the time he finished all this, it was a few minutes past nine. The class was already in progress when he arrived. He handed the receipt to the teacher and took a seat.

The class was reviewing the first person singular of irregular verbs. The teacher, a tall woman with long red hair, was going around the room, one student at a time. Kaiser's turn came as soon as he got into his desk and opened his book.

Señor . . . The instructor looked at the receipt. Señor Kaiser. She looked at the list of irregular verbs and made a selection.

Ver, she said.

Ver, Kaiser said. To see. His mouth was dry and his tongue was thick. *Veo. Yo veo. Veo.*

THE END